I0554271

THE WEDDING BED
Nicolas Buchele

CALIGULA PRESS

For Fer

Prescience is in itself creation. An event, once announced, exists. It is fact, and although it is still to come it is more real and more significant than something that has already happened.

Tiziano Terzani, *A Fortune Teller Told Me*

Part 1

1.

The supreme councillor's dreams have lately been troubling him. They have been a lucid instrument throughout the years, ever more lucid as he has grown less mobile, and now that he spends all his days recumbent, more or less, and all his recumbent days dreaming, more or less, they feel like a far better means of travel than the clumsy material vehicles. In his dreams, he soars and swoops, eagle-fashion, rising on thermals to the highest point above the land where breath may still be drawn, or gliding so low above the surface that he can make out the slightest movement in the smallest grain of clod. But he is also a rat, or rabbit, burrowing, an earthworm, an ant; he is a jellyfish, billowing, a shark, pouncing; he is all creatures and none; he has knowledge of all deeds, understanding of all motives. He sees, he hears, above all he feels. Oh, beautiful—the rich warm feeling that ripples through him as he dreams, recumbent, of this nation, its hopes, fears, desires and demands, its clamour, rattle and hum, its endless, tinny, ring-around song.

His earthly carcass, however, is unmistakably a toad. A beautiful bloated pink toad, silky of skin, enormous of wart and wattle. He has not seen his feet these many years except in a mirror: they are huge, his feet, they bulge at the end of his enormous legs, and are all but useless to him now. Once a week comes a little brown man and buffs them for him, filing at horn and snipping at skin, a beautiful ticklish affair that sends him chuckling to sleep. He wiggles his toes now, in the gentle breeze of the fan—he thinks of his toes as little balloons tethered to the hams of his feet—though he cannot tell if any movement travels through his vast recumbent frame to the extremities. It is all the same to him: to have lived, he thinks, chuckling, it is enough to have wiggled in the mind.

To say that his dreams have been troubling him is to say a great deal, for nothing troubles the supreme councillor. He reclines on a magnificent bed—you would call it a wedding bed, though the supreme councillor has never married, and has no plans to marry now, at this late stage in his earthly existence. The thought of going a-wooing sends mirth rippling from the ticklish soles of his unseen feet to the top of his hairless head. Perhaps he might take a fancy to the daughter of an influential family; there are so many, and they are so influential, little princely houses every one, with their Palladian villas that occupy every last inch of the land on which they stand, and the washing machine at the top of the great winding marble stairs. Perhaps he could have himself taken there on a bier, on the shoulders of four burly farmers, gifts of gold arranged all around his recumbent form— Would his suit be welcome? He believes it would. Oh, it would be very welcome indeed.

There was in his day a fellow whose name escapes him, as all names do, though his memory is as sharp as it ever was— There was in his day a fellow nicknamed the Frog, who in his dotage overthrew the main wife and took up with a plain farmgirl of fifteen or so, who was some kind of servant in the fellow's house and was nicknamed the Little Fish, and atop their wedding cake, at their well-attended, much-publicised wedding, sat a little sugar sculpture of a frog kissing a fish—

And the besotted fellow, who was incontinent at least in the verbal department, let it be known that, though he was in his dotage, sex with the Little Fish was the best he had ever had. Perhaps it would have been. But it did not last, for the Little Fish took a fancy to one of the burly farmers who carried the

6

Frog's bier, with rippling muscles and a cheerful, open face, and the burly farmer under cover of night slew the Frog, and the Little Fish became a very rich widow before she was out of her teens. Well, it did not last, for the Frog's grown children from his first marriage made a clamour and ruckus, and the farmer was taken into custody, and the Little Fish with him, and so—

Did they let them out again? It is very likely they did, for nothing ever ends here, though what became of the pair has momentarily slipped the supreme councillor's mind. No matter. It is for the universal lesson that he rehearses the tale to himself. Which is what? No fool like an old fool? He believes himself to be very old—oh, older than anyone can remember—and no fool at all. Perhaps it is not for the lesson at all, but for the buttery joy of the tale itself that he rehearses it.

Because now he is troubled, and he does not much like to be troubled. Recumbent there in his cushions on the wedding bed, which is richly carved around the frame with birds and flowers and little processions of wise men in conical hats about God knows what business, and gilded, and lacquered, and put together without a nail lest the cold iron pierce marital harmony, he dreams troubling dreams. Or not dreams so much as one dream, always the same, advancing, day after day, night after night. The cast is quite familiar.

What draws him there the supreme councillor does not know. He has the run of the land, yet day after day, night after night, as he glides about in search of some fresh diversion, the nocturnal country spread out below him, the black winding rivers, the jungle darkly breathing, the great high-risers sparkling like a forest of mobile phones, he feels the tug. It is a strange, sour, metallic tug, somewhere in his bowels, a kind of vertigo, an urge and need, and no matter how he struggles— or no, that too is wrong, he does not struggle, though he knows he could: it is rather that in spite of himself he does not

—

7

then wish to go anywhere else. And with a great whoosh he nosedives from his eagle height, as if down a chute or sock, and with a flat knock as of bone hitting wood, there he is.

Always in the old hut. He does not need to look around to know from the piercing smell of mould and wet ash and washing powder that he is back in the old hut. Also a note of stagnant shit and vegetable decay from the canal that runs somewhere nearby. A concrete walkway runs along it; that way you gain the road. He can taste the iron of the railing on his tongue. Across the still flat black water, vines droop from an overgrown lot. Sometimes, with a roar as if its guts were being torn from its belly, a canal boat bears down on you, passes, and rips up two great roots of grey-green water in its wake. Vacant eyes stare through you from the weakly illuminated cabin, where wage slaves sit on low benches, their day nearly done.

The woman's day, by contrast, is just beginning. In three plastic bowls, one pink, one baby blue, one whitish with a suggestion of floral pattern in its depth, her breakfast is arrayed. Rice, a little grilled fish, a soup of dark green vegetables and stringy bamboo shoots. Sweat beads her forehead, for the soup is very hot, as is the sauce of chopped peppers and fermented fish she spoons over the mackerel to mask its metallic tang. Behind her eyes—oh, beautiful—she feels hot, bright and clear, as if they were floating in pure spirit. On the other hand, her bones ache, and her toes flex and unflex on the floor, which is covered in two kinds of patterned PVC, one pink and floral, one white and geometric, cigarette burns punctuating them like welts, and over by the bed a piece

8

has torn away to show the damp board underneath.

These spots are all familiar to the supreme councillor, and he greets them like friends. Also a kind of electric prickle in her shoulder blades. Hello, hello. Also the boil on her right cheek, which does not seem to want to go away, and feels hard and tight when she stretches her mouth, to smile or otherwise. The leaden makeup flakes there to expose the fierce red spot, no matter how often you retouch. But if it cannot be made beautiful, it can be made unimportant; it is only at the beginning of every day that she finds it, with a droop of mild disappointment, still there.

Hello to the plastic bags full of belongings, arrayed on nails along the wall; the trousers and skirts in one, the tops in another, the underwear in a third. A fourth holds the two good little dresses. Hello to the bad shoes. Hello to a pile of clothes that, neatly folded, awaits washing: this will be done in the long hours of the morning, not now. For now she spoons her breakfast into her mouth, hunched over cross-legged, the neck stretched as far as it will go, gulping, slurping, almost as if she were force-feeding herself.

It pleases the supreme councillor to see her keeping her strength up—or perhaps it is he who is keeping her strength up. Does she know he is here? He is not aware of any reciprocal penetration, if it is penetration that makes him seem to feel what she seems to be thinking. Yet she is careful in her observances to such spirits as she seems to believe occupy the premises and surrounds. Perhaps one of the mulberry woodbines she lays out on a little saucer is really for him, or the shot glass of rum, or the incense she lights, now she has done the best that she can by her breakfast. Well, he neither smokes nor drinks, and incense makes his eyes water, but he is grateful for the kind thought.

It sometimes seems to the supreme councillor that kind thoughts alone are keeping him alive, at his enormous age. It is certainly not exercise, nor for all he can remember food, though he has a notion that he sometimes takes a spluttering sip of lime-water, from a beaker held to his mouth by a flunkey. How they fuss; he wishes they would not fuss. Is he fasting, he wonders, that they should be so concerned? Has he gone on some kind of hunger strike? Yet his body is vast and pink, in the pink of health, and he has never, when he had to rise, not risen to the occasion. Not that he is very clear when he was last required to rise; it may be days, or weeks, or years. He knows only, from the warm golden complacency coursing through his veins, that he is in the pink of health, and ready to rise to any occasion—

He believes that his toad-body is slowly turning to gold, and that the veins have already accomplished the transubstantiation. Has he begun to glow? And the well-wishers, with their kind thoughts, are they brought awe-struck, on tiptoe, to his wedding bed, and are the gauze or muslin curtains sometimes parted by the breeze from the fan, to grant them a fleeting glimpse of his magnificent recumbent form?

He at any rate feels them, feels their kind wishes, and in turn wishes them well. And this poor troubling, troubled woman too. He wishes her fingers well, with their incessant nervous motion; they are like little fleet nocturnal rodents, her fingers, busily, skilfully nibbling away at their tasks. See how briskly they spoon the leftovers into the baby-blue bowl, and stack it neatly on top of the others. See how efficiently they unlatch the door, unscrew a water bottle, and rinse themselves over the two boards that form a kind of landing over the walkway. And now, door once again latched securely, how intent these fingers are on retrieving, from a little Tupperware box under a loose floorboard, the utensils. It is these fingers too, with their chipped purple-black varnish and chewed nail beds, that have fashioned the utensils, in the long hours of the morning. Lighters, minus the metal enclosure, their funnels narrowed by means of nail varnish or toothpick splint; slim straws rolled from cigarette packets; strips of tin foil, peeled off the paper that once attached to them, except for a short piece at the end to make a little holder. She picks out one that, already moulded into a flat-bottomed boat, holds a blackish-brown smear.

'Titanic,' she whispers to herself.

The joke never fails to amuse the supreme councillor, no matter how often repeated. There runs a background theme of sinking boats through this culture, which has produced a great many fishermen and no seafarers at all. The fear of seasonally swollen waters; the horror of the deep. These are alluvial lands, and in swamps like this, for all that the slum huddles against the side of a great office tower, it has a special poignancy. Ah, he thinks as the lighter snicks and a point of blue-gold flame is snatched from the air to settle demurely a good half-centimetre above the funnel, perhaps that is why I return. Or again perhaps he only thrills to the accomplishment of this small ritual, the casual dovetailing of complex skills.

The dark smear in the foil now swells to a rich bubbling chocolatey soup, and the woman sucks the thin beard of bone-white smoke into a paper straw and inhales. She holds the smoke in, and in one practised sequence lets go of the lighter, rips the straw from her mouth and spits, from behind her teeth and into her palm, a coin on which a yellow-white deposit has formed like a dirty snow drift. The whole manoeuvre is rather like an awakening bat suddenly spreading its wings and baring its fangs. She hisses out a fat billowing cloud, sinks back, and for the first time tonight seems for a moment at peace.

2.

The minister steps out of the lift, trailed by a gaggle of officials. They are remarkably like geese, waddling and jostling, rubbernecking, chattering and hissing for his attention. Also the incontinence of their cloaca. He snuffles. Really he must try to get this levity under control. In his antechamber the petitioners are already waiting. One of his few indulgences is to take the front way into the office first thing, for a swift review of the petitioners, of whom in this country there is rarely a dearth. When he leaves, he takes the back door.

Today's petitioners are a group of indistinct middle-aged persons, dressed in stiff Sunday silks except for one large, brown, ungainly schoolgirl with thick spectacles and enormous thighs and feet, and a familiar figure whose comfortable bulk gives the impression of having been sown into the uniform. Presently they come to a kind of attention, and the minister raises his hands and lowers his head in a greeting of such becoming humility that for a moment he looks like the smallest man in the room. Barely stopping, he promises to be with them in no time.

He has no pressing business and could be with them straight away, but that would disappoint them. They have made it this far and will wish to taste their privilege to the full by waiting a little longer.

In the office, he takes up position behind the desk, under the tall gilt-framed portraits, and waves for his attaché case. One of the more ceremonially minded officials slowly pulls the doors to, two-handed, bowing at the waist. No doubt a homosexual, with the concomitant need to serve. Over his head, the minister catches the uniformed man's eye in the antechamber, and gives the barest wink. The man returns a hint of a smile before the great doors fully close on him.

The men now line up in front of the desk; only his secretary stands politely aside. The parade, with its echoes of a police-station muster, is an important part of their day.

'Ah,' barks the minister, looking up from his desk as if it had never happened before. 'Was there anything?'

They shuffle and shake their heads.

'Well then,' he says and adds the ceremonial phrase: 'Today we shall work hard. Meeting at—' He looks at his chief of staff.

'Ten-thirty,' the chief of staff says.

'*Rare*,' he says by way of dismissal, a harsh sound strangled in his crow throat, and yet a pure sound too, untainted by any emotion at all. As they turn to leave he sits down. A good part of his day is taken up with these charades; that he has not let his senses become blunted to them is an article of pride with him. High office, he has seen it too often, fattens the brain, which soon squats like a bullfrog on the spine, bloated, honking out is monotonous song while all around the waters rise.

He riffles through papers, then indicates the petitioners. 'What do they want?'

The secretary shrugs. 'To express gratitude,' he ventures.

The minister sighs. The merit of these cases is assessed somewhere in the bowels of the operation. He gets up again to admit the petitioners, in the expression, *personally*. He recalls the wife of an underling who, trapped in conversation with him at some function, was moved to describe the venue as 'very exclusive, inside and out.' Stifling hilarity, he opens the doors. The petitioners snap to once more.

'Ah,' he says. 'Come, come.'

They duck their heads as they file past him into the office where, despite nudges from the uniformed man, they regroup such a long way from the desk that it would be impossible for the minister to take his seat there. So be it; they will do this standing up. The schoolgirl, solidly anchored in her boat-like shoes, is clutching a vast hamper of fruit and processed foods. There is always, for no reason he can discover, a bumper jar of powdered coffee whitener among the victuals. They will be distributed among the menial staff later on.

The girl, he suspects, is meant to represent Youth; he hopes she will not launch into song. Unmusical himself, the minister has no time for any kind of amateur performance. Only once, in his daughter's early school years, was he inveigled to attend a Father's Day event, where the assembled parents chattered blithely over the interminable caterwauling of other people's children but were transported into a frenzy of pride and adoration by that of their own. And now, he winces to remember, his daughter is to be a bride.

A woman in stiff purple silks has begun to address him. She gives a great impression of squareness, from the components of her suit to the shape of the face and spectacles, as if she had been modularly assembled. Yet her theme is his daring. She speaks of how grateful the mothers of this country are—a simper tells him that she is a mother too—for his *daring* initiatives in bringing order to society. Especially to Youth. The schoolgirl gurns and stares out of the window, oblivious to the reference. If that is the daughter then the father must be a hefty fellow, no doubt a provincial thug who, having come to wealth and influence, is now doubly afraid of losing it all to men like his former self. Still, it is such men who deliver the provincial vote.

The minister smiles thinly.

Emboldened, the woman recalls the way stations of his campaign. Her voice has a slight edge, as if she is willing her words to be true. The minister recognizes one of the grey men in the background as a former army general associated with the dark events of a decade ago, though on which side he does not remember. What can he want? A return to favour, if indeed he ever lost it? Such enormous complications attend on the simplest encounters. A man might have his task cut out bringing all these divergent forces into lockstep.

The woman has got up to his *daring* intervention a couple of weeks ago, when he descended for the TV cameras on an immense new entertainment district and shut it down for the night. He recalls it with pleasure. The vast fronts of those entertainment hangars, lit up in brilliant neon colours. His nation's infatuation with the brightest of bright lights at night, the fairy lamps you see adorning the humblest hut. Searchlights scanned the sky. And the huge scale, more suited to the industrial production of large armaments, perhaps fighter bombers. Underscoring the aviation theme was a pair of giant windsocks in slick pink parachute silk that tumesced and detumesced atop a flight of ceremonial stairs. How efficiently the customers were marshalled there, with the aid of hundreds of movable barriers.

Down the wide avenue he marched, ringingly, ahead of a battalion of senior officers, with his brisk, short, high-stepping gait. Though his own days in the force are long past, he has the heels of his shoes reinforced, for the pleasure of hearing them ring out in the corridors over which he reigns, and to leave the apparatus in no doubt that its master is here. Flashlights went off, television lamps made him a shining beacon for his troops. The officers, too, proved efficient in appropriating the barriers, when he stopped outside the most popular establishment on the strip.

The workaday fluorescent lights flickered on inside as he took up position, framed against a mass of bedraggled youngsters who were being herded out into the improvised corral. A toyshop of microphones assembled under his chin, and he addressed the nation in simple words: a dry, thin, reasonable stand-in for the moral majority.

He spoke of the importance of leisure, and the importance of moderation; of pleasure and duty. Officers released a group of youngsters into the circle of reporters. The girls were practically naked, nothing but a sort of large kerchief protecting their modesty, tied at the back with a couple of strings, and the shortest of hotpants below. They could not have been older than sixteen and were hopelessly trying to pull the available textile over their exposed puppy fat. The boys, knuckled and chicken-haired, grinned gormlessly, afraid for their lives.

Under a strafe of flashlights, he was a kindly uncle. Kindly but firm. He asked about their parents. He asked about their parents' feelings. He spoke to them of our obligations to our elders. Their toes drew circles on the tarmac. One of the girls began to cry.

Knowing tears to be the argument that overrides all others, he swiftly terminated the interview, shielding the girl from the reporters as if it had been they who brought forth this overflow of confused emotion. Gently, shaking one raised finger, he scolded the weeping girl. The picture was on all front pages the next day. For the girl, too, it was beneficial, because it forced her to accept him as a substitute parent. Immediately she calmed and soon began to smile. Only then did he permit his officers to lead the youngsters away. In later press interviews they all testified to his kindness.

The woman peters out and raises her hands. The minister mutters thanks and is about to usher the petitioners to the official sofas when another figure steps forward. A sleek black animal seems to have died on top of the fellow's bloodless old head. He is if anything even humbler than the minister, but when he speaks, barely above a whisper, in slow phrases resonant with courtly tradition, his voice has an actor's effortless reach. He expresses the customary gratitude for the minister's activities. In this country it is considered a great sacrifice if a man does any kind of work, even as it would be thought unconscionable if he failed to put in long ineffectual hours—especially in the upper reaches of public service, which have long been as a reward for effort in other fields, a place to put up the feet.

A gentleman from an old family, it strikes the minister; but what does that signify? If he were of real consequence he would not be among these petitioners but find another way of troubling him. Sidelined then, passed over. Or merely old: the skin of his face looks like a mildewed rag. Perhaps glad to have been asked along to any sort of gathering. Or incautious with his investments, ever a bracing tonic. The pieces will fall into place soon enough.

For now, the man treats the minister to an orotund paraphrase of his own remarks to the press, on the subject of duty. Clearly he has struck a chord in the withered heart.

'And—' the old man begins again.

With a thud, something crumbles away in the ranks of the petitioners, like a pothole opening after long rains. The schoolgirl has dropped the propitiatory hamper: not so solidly parked after all. In their efforts to help her pick up the spilt victuals, the petitioners look as if they too are about to tumble into the pit. The minister stifles hilarity. The girl has fallen to her knees like a rag doll, and the skirt has ridden up her oaken thighs. She starts to weep.

Seizing his opportunity, the minister cuts through the group and loops around, grips the girl's elbow with one hand and the square mother's—even her bottom is square—by the other, and as the girl struggles to her feet he steers them to the official sofa. In the nape of his solicitously bent neck he can feel a prickle of respect, for his humility, and for his kindness.

Once the girl is seated he allows himself a chuckle; all but mother and daughter join gratefully in. The accident has broken the ice, and now everyone speaks at once. The small misfortunes of others are a great source of enjoyment for his countrymen; hence the many Down's people and dwarves on television, with their duck voices, their quick repartee—

'*Rare*,' says the minister, motioning for them to sit down freely about the suite. The titled old fellow sinks into the upholstery with a soft sigh. There is a great deal of shuffling and shifting and adjusting of clothes over ageing flesh and bone. Suit jackets are being unbuttoned, trouser legs hitched, skirts smoothed. Amused consolation is being offered, for the girl not to take the mishap so much to heart. She relishes the attention, through her tears. That, the minister supposes, is the flipside of their ready *schadenfreude*, which is really no more than complacency. In fiercer parts of the continent the girl would no doubt have to kill herself, but here they look at her fondly now, as a kind of lightning conductor for the perpetual cosmic subversion of our best efforts. But perhaps they are getting a little carried away.

'Now—' The uniformed man speaks for the first time. A deep, rich, oiled, authoritative voice. 'We should put our case. The time—'

'—is short,' cuts in the grey former general, who has kept quiet amid the commotion.

'Oh, time—' the minister demurs.

These few words restore purpose to the group. No one appeals to the old man to resume; he is spent, tucked away. Instead, the former general takes the floor. He has a gruff clerical manner, and his hair stands in short bristles on his head, a compromise between soldier and monk. Taking up the theme of *daring*, he adds to it the theme of *leadership*. The great buzzword of the time: young leaders are forever being brought together under one heading or another—sport, business, science—and shipped to seaside resorts in the off-season, where they spend the days milling and half-listening to inspirational addresses, and the nights lounging and singing sentimental songs. In the newspapers, lists of leaders in their field, ranked in numerical order, have become a regular feature.

It is the view of the petitioners (says the general) that the minister has exhibited commendable *leadership* in the quest to bring order to society, in the return to *values* that for too long—

The general, the minister remembers now, was in the dark days believed to have stood on the side of reform, one of very few senior officers to be so placed. He was but a middle-ground figure at the time, and the minister a humble administrator in the force. It was only after events had taken their bloody and inconclusive turn that the general came to widespread attention by retiring very publicly from the Army, not to go into politics as so many do, but rather to embrace religion. He went, it was said, into the forest. That explains his grey tunic; the sect under whose spell he has fallen believes in austerity, of dress and demeanour, and is broadly opposed to the killing of living creatures. Perhaps, thinks the austere minister, they regard me as a natural ally. Though what sect on earth believes in excess?

Only recently has the general emerged from his long sulk, to take part in certain panel discussions, under the aegis of certain publicly funded organizations, on the question of restoring *values* to a society everywhere beset by foreign influence and moral decay, which many consider one and the same. This view is not shared by the minister, who understands history as a play of equal but opposing forces and sets no great store by the moral standards of the past, which on closer inspection often merely prove a more brazen kind of hypocrisy, or an absence of records about the slovenly conduct of the masses, as the case may be. He has been careful not to advertise that view.

As citizens who share the minister's goals (the general concludes) the petitioners have this day come to express their gratitude, and their support, and also to give courage—he uses the homely term as a parent might—to one whose *daring* efforts and *leadership* in this struggle have left an indelible mark in the minds of many, who for their part hope to see more of this *daring*, and this *leadership*, in the years to come.

The others nod assent, like wooden puppets.

The room suddenly darkens, and into the silence that follows the general's summing-up falls the sound of distant pebbles striking tin, which swells within seconds to an almighty rush of water.

'It is raining,' muses the old fellow. 'The plants are grateful.'

The schoolgirl, recovered, giggles.

3.

'Out of the question,' says the minister.

They are alone now in the tall gloomy office, he and the uniformed man, whom he considers his best and oldest friend. His friend sits comfortably, at ease, commanding in any setting. This has always been an interesting trait to the minister, who is devoid of charisma himself. The great, soft, limpid eyes, with their unfathomable depth. The ability to silence underlings with the slightest turn of the head.

The friend turns his hand palm up as who should say, if you are sure—

'Oh, absolutely out of the question.' The minister guffaws, though in truth the morning's hilarity has gone out of him. 'To begin with, there is the money.'

'Ah money, money—'

'You have thought about it.'

His friend smiles and shrugs. His official position does not match the influence he is believed to wield: a humble superintendent of police, he presides over perhaps the most profitable district in the capital, and thus the nation, but has not risen as far as many predicted. And yet it is for his support that more outwardly ambitious officers first appeal. A great stilled force, that is the impression he gives. Even in their youth, he seemed to move only half as much as everyone else.

'In the whole history of this nation there has never been a Leader with such deep pockets,' says the minister.

'One man, with deep pockets,' says the superintendent. 'Yet others have pockets too.'

'And they are where?' says the minister irritably.

'Everywhere.'

'Precisely. They are not in one place, as our Leader is, but scattered all over the shop. That is how we beat them.'

'We?'

'I am a loyal member of his government.'

The superintendent inclines his head a fraction. His eyes are all soft depth, rather like those of a faithful Rottweiler, who will rip a man to shreds the moment he is let off the chain.

'I did not see,' says the minister, 'among these—comedians you brought here today, with their hamper—'

The superintendent gives a small snort.

'Quite. I did not see among them even one capable of drumming up a fraction of the money that would be required—'

'They are the vanguard,' says the superintendent.

'Ah.' The minister throws up his hands and leans back in the vinyl.

'They are the public,' says the superintendent.

'In this country,' says the minister, 'we have not one public but many. We have those who vote on their own prejudices, and those who are herded into the booth. We have those who cheer their side like a football team, and those who are bought one by one. We have those in search of a fresh diversion, and those who back a winner—'

'And I brought you one of each.'

The minister barks another laugh. 'A veritable cross-section.'

His friend leans forward a fraction, or perhaps only permits his bulk to loom a little larger. 'Do not underestimate the general. He has not been seen for some years, but he has been felt.'

'By whom? The tree frogs?'

'Ah.' The superintendent turns to the windows, where sunlight sparkles in fat droplets dripping *rat-tat-tat* from the ledge. 'You know everything.'

The minister relents. 'No. I am sure you are right. But even supposing—'

'Nor,' says the superintendent, still looking out the window, 'his Excellency.'

'The old man in the wig? Never seen him before.'

His friend names a name.

'My God. He has—'

'As I say, the vanguard.' He turns to face him. 'One of each.'

'Not quite of each.' Youth, reluctantly represented by a gurning lump of a schoolgirl, and of the younger aspiring classes, to whom so much frantic building activity all over the city is owing, to say nothing of the nameless millions in menial work: not a trace. Their greed, their resentment, their stupidity—that is the tidal wave on which the Leader has been carried to power. In a way he embodies them. 'All of a certain age, yes?'

The superintendent fixes his eyes on him. 'Of an age where they can be depended on to go to the polls. The rest—'

'We are a young country.'

'Listen, please.' The superintendent stays calmly intent. 'I was going to say: the rest will have to be won over. So?'

'There is your flaw,' says the minister. 'Even were I to mount a challenge, as they—as you—seem to want me to do, the Leader is at the peak of his popularity.'

'So are you.'

'By my lights.'

'We both know that your lights are—'

'Lights, I am talking about. We have now, in this city, the biggest LCD billboard on the continent. No doubt it can be seen from space. We have more mobile phones per head than any other country. Yet we are none of us more than two generations from peasants.'

'None?'

'*His Excellency* is a relic,' the minister snaps.

'Relics are revered. But I was thinking of you.'

'My parents had a hardware store. And their parents before them.'

'Hardly one store. Hardly peasants.'

'Same. Peasants, shopkeepers. We are dazzled, is my point.'

'Ah,' the superintendent smiles complacently. 'You think for me. We can be dazzled, and none more easily than those young people you worry about. They may prove the least of your problems.'

The minister grunts. 'And what would I run on?'

'Your theme is—'

'—order, yes.'

'Social order.'

'Order, order, order. That is not enough. That is already my theme, you cannot hope to win people over by harping on something you are already doing. You need a coup.'

The superintendent's eyes widen for a moment, then he breathes out softly. 'That could be—'

'Not that kind,' the minister snaps. 'We have had enough of those. A—coup. A stroke. A strike. No, make that three.'

'Three strikes,' the superintendent says comfortably. 'Beautiful. Each of a different flavour. Tic and tac and toe. We start with—'

There comes a solemn knock on the door.

'Come,' barks the minister.

His chief of staff, to remind him that it is time for the meeting.

'Good.' His friend rises with some effort and pats him lightly on the arm.

'You are fat,' says the minister.

The superintendent spreads his hands what-can-you-do? 'That is what my wife says,' he says. They smile mechanically: it is a great joke in this country that all men are afraid of their

25

wives, especially those who are not; an article of faith really. 'You on the other hand are handsome and slim.'

The minister dismisses the compliment. 'It is *metabolism*,' he says using the foreign word.

The superintendent is silent for a moment, then: 'Ah!' and a formulaic 'Now I am going.' He raises his hands in a swift greeting, as if sheltering a small bird. 'We will speak again.'

The minister lifts his hands in a sketched response. 'We will speak, but you have my answer.'

He meets with senior civil servants, who brief him on progress in his campaigns. They address him through little bendy conference microphones, as if about to fellate the devices, despite sitting only a few feet away. Really he finds it easier to hear the nervous ones who forget to push the button, since no electronics distort their voice. Deafness, the family curse. One day he will have to look into the question who benefited from the purchase of this useless job lot. No doubt the answer is known to everyone here.

The results are neither satisfactory nor unsatisfactory. Closing time is being enforced. Urine samples are being taken. Colossal fines are being collected, though how much of the money will find its way into state coffers is a question these reports cannot answer. Presently a blubber-lipped permanent under-secretary who gives the impression of having been inflated with a bicycle pump starts droning on about efforts in the southern provinces, excepting those subject to the emergency decree and the autonomous administration, etc., etc. Projecting reptilian inscrutability, the minister lets his mind wander.

The task at hand is to persuade the supreme councillor to officiate at his daughter's wedding. His wife has left him in no doubt about the urgency of the matter. Any less illustrious personage would shame their ancestors.

The minister does not believe his own ancestors would be troubled one way or the other. They were closed, hard, industrious people who kept their eyes firmly on the ground — literally in the case of his mother, who towards the end was so bent over with arthritis that she could barely lift her head above chest height. And yet almost to the end she insisted on dragging herself from box to box through the damp murky store house, with its cat-piss miasma, its fungal infestations, where she knew the whereabouts of every nut and plunger; and on feast days, almost to the end, she placed the pig's head on the ceremonial table with her own clawed hands.

Meanwhile his father, mute and drooling since his stroke, could only be calmed in the fretting of his good arm if he was wheeled to the front so he could watch the loading and unloading of the great diesel lorries, which he had for so long directed with his guttural shouts. *Rare!* That is almost the minister's earliest sound memory, followed by the clank of machine parts that, even in his childhood, were forever having to be replaced after an overland trip. In those days the roads were not what they are today, but as the roads got better the lorries got older, so the amount of maintenance stayed the same throughout his youth. For all he knows his sister operates these monsters still. He must remember to ask her, if she can be persuaded to abandon her command post for the wedding day. A humourless woman, his sister, who will no doubt sniff out an implied slight of her business acumen when he puts the question. That alone will make it worthwhile.

The wife's side, on the other hand, had a big new house on the edge of town, with glazed turquoise roof tiles and a cod-Palladian portal, which took up the whole plot of land on which it stood. It was said that the birds would not fly over it but made a respectful detour. It was not kindly meant. Still, they were shrewd enough people—none shrewder than his wife who, he knows, has kept certain investments and acquisitions from him over the years that will be enough to keep the family for a generation, should something happen to him. Early in his career, when he still wore the uniform, she had a lively business on the side. His lipless mouth softens when he recalls them now, those days of hard graft and ambition. They were a team then, in their way, though of course he put a stop to her activities when they grew incompatible with his position.

The South is a lazy backwater, where nothing much changes from one decade to the next. Such extraordinary long quiet dusks in the monsoon, with the monumental clouds piling into the sky, and the ground still aglow like a jewel for long minutes after the sun has gone. All the odder that the inflated fellow—a native son—should be going on about it so interminably. The smaller the infractions, and the smaller their number, the more the man seems determined to break them down into even smaller units. A handful of arrests here, a poorish collection of fines there, a group of monks caught at cards among the rubber trees: it has little reach, his campaign in the South. There is no vice to speak of except at the border, and of course it is there that least of all is being done.

Well, let him crawl down his columns, there is no point setting his blubber lips a-tremble now. Even in the remotest villages, boys doctor their scooters and break their necks, and business rivals shoot each other in the head. No effort is wholly wasted, even there.

There was never a question that he would take over the business. He believes that was unusual for the time. Once his parents saw him excel at school beyond whatever expectations they had, they took one of the abrupt and immutable decisions characteristic of their race and willed the business to his sister, without even bothering to adopt a son-in-law. They simply announced that he was henceforth to be left to his studies and would do them proud. His sister was exquisitely torn in her emotions, and remains so to this day. Was she to exult in her inheritance of the family firm, or was she to resent him for being indulged? She is a female version of him, thin-lipped, hard-knuckled, no airs perhaps, but also no graces. Without the business, what would she have had to look forward to? She does not even like cats.

The parents, too, knew nothing of social niceties. His mother-in-law emerged from the dowry negotiations white around the nostrils and somehow shrunken in her splendid starched silks, leaning heavily on her husband's arm. Still, the wife's parents must have got a fair amount, for they paid half the fees for his LL.M overseas plus the rent on a small flat on the outskirts of the ancient university town. By and by they came to see him as a propellant to social ascent and, had they lived, would have relished their son-in-law's rise to high office—as their due, perhaps, but relished it all the same. He does not blame the wife for inheriting this trait, by nature or nurture, either which; it is only correct that she should tend the ancestral flame.

The task before him, at any rate, is to persuade the supreme councillor to preside at his daughter's wedding. That will be another milestone and also, he supposes, a fine measure of his popularity, now at its height. An extraordinary man, the supreme councillor. No one he has spoken to can recall a single achievement to which he might owe his eminent

29

position, yet there are hints of profound insight into the nation's soul, of a deep fecund knowledge acquired in unmentionable ways.

The supreme councillor's people, as powdered and perfumed a bunch of toadies as ever lived, have hinted to the minister's people that His Excellency might smile on the request, provided certain conditions are met. They did not stop to specify these conditions before drawing the curtains again, as it were, around the great man's recumbent form.

It is understood that after a decent interval an offer will be made. He will ask his own associates what amount of moneys and land would be considered acceptable, then offer half. Part of the interest the minister takes in the transaction is to see whether he can expose the supreme councillor, even if only to his own eyes, as the greedy fat toad he undoubtedly is. There is barely a national park across the country, or so it is said, on which the supreme councillor and his people have not in one way or another encroached. A love of forests and mountains, of jungly seclusion. Scratch the surface—

The minister is keenly aware of his prejudices, or his judgements. His own people were shriven centuries ago of this tendency to retreat into primal nature. Not for them the low murmuring among the foliage, the glowing embers, the screech and rasp of unseen fauna in the impenetrable darkness. Not for them the formless slide into sleep. Effort, yes. Coastal inlets, trading posts. The general store. Wherever the forces of natural disorder could be sufficiently subdued to facilitate commerce and regular hours. None of this dissolute monkeying about—

He calls himself to order. How long has this silence been going on? He can feel anxious minds working, behind a dozen pairs of eyes fixed in his direction. Pens hang suspended in mid-air. Mouths breathe.

'Yes, well,' says the minister. 'These reports—' he allows the suspense to rise a little further. 'They are in their way well and good. You have worked hard to compile them, you and your staff.' They are tensing for the *but*, like strings for the twanging. 'The results, however: I had hoped for bolder action. Had you not?' He looks around, eliciting a few timid nods, which may well mean nothing at all. 'Did we not all hope that some of these—*problems* would by now—' Yes, that is for the moment the way to play it. Take them along into shared disappointment. 'Like me, I am sure you are sad'—he uses the homely word—'that no bolder progress has been made, that some of the officers in the field have, in some instances, disappointed us.' The nods are vigorously indignant now.

'I believed we had made it clear, to all officers, that we hoped for action across the board, even where that would be painful, even where such action would require sacrifices from the officers in the field, with regard to their—their *livelihood*, in some instances. But perhaps I was wrong. Perhaps we all underestimated the difficulty of the task we have taken on together. Mindsets are not soon changed; old habits are not soon broken—'

The minister has them well on side now, down to the tumescent son of the South, who looks fit to pop with feigned eagerness. 'But it is the task that has fallen upon us, and to which we have, willy-nilly, committed ourselves. We have given long hours and hard work to this task, which has fallen upon us. It has not been enough. Longer hours, harder work, will be required to accomplish it.' He raises a knuckly fist. 'But accomplish it, gentlemen, we shall. We shall be firm, we shall work harder. When we meet again'—he once more looks into each face in turn—'we shall see better results.'

He sits for a moment in silence. Then: *'Rare!'* and a nod and he gets up and marches out of the room. Behind him, relief ebbs like a long slow wave on the beach at eventide.

4.

They are fussing again. What is it now? Perhaps if the supreme councillor were to observe them closely, he would see a pattern in their fussing, like the changing of the tides, or the changing of the guards, which in some distant past he may have commanded, in some capacity or other now lost in the depths of his capacious memory. Only an effort of great will, a sort of mental climbing down of stairways and opening of heavy doors and scanning of long shelves can retrieve these facts. He pictures himself on a ladder, blowing dust off a great red volume in which the data have been entered in careful copperplate. Brown spots riddle the musty pages— No. The time when he relied on facts is past, and he has no desire, at this late stage in his earthly existence, to go hopping round that treadmill again.

His chuckle seems to have alarmed the attendants, whose tension he can feel all the way from inside his dreams. Oh, but they mean well, they are kindly disposed towards him and want his best. And they shall not have it! He chuckles again, prompting another great tremulous wave of concern from the attendants. Ah well. Best to let them get on with it. It is, this, perhaps neither the changing of the guards, nor the changing of the tides, but the changing of the sheets.

But how extraordinary, that one so inactive should have had such a distinguished career, to judge among other things by the medals that once adorned his enormously bulging chest, and would adorn it again were he to don the sandy uniform once more. He has every confidence that the attendants keep it in good order, if not in expectation of his

---

33

imminent re-emergence then by way of tending the shrine.

Listen: what is a good soldier but one who keeps the peace? If he did not earn every last medal, such as the Lion Crest for bravery in wartime, second left top row, he certainly earned a great many of them, by having no truck with hostilities of any kind, nor discharging a firearm in anger, nor overseeing such discharge, that he can remember. Yes, there has been no one like him for keeping the peace. That is perhaps why he is now turning to gold: so that when he departs this life, a century or two from now, men may worship the aurified husk. Perhaps they will erect a Temple of the Golden Toad on the site of this official residence, where worshippers may come and pray for peace. They will think of appropriate offerings, he has no fear on that score.

Like all the greatest careers in this nation, his has been built on no achievement that anyone can recall. Nor he himself, for great achievements, he has long believed, are nothing but terrible disruptions in the flow of affairs, deep rents in the fabric of time that it can take long miserable years of penance to mend, if they can be mended at all. Conquest, resettlement: these are but two of the names of Pain, whose name is legion. To have served entirely without distinction, by contrast, as he has, that strikes him now as the greatest achievement of all.

And yet he is humble, and grateful, for he was guided in all things not by ambition, nor by thirst for glory, nor by calculation and intellectual pride, but by the golden light from above that, if you wanted to speak its name, could perhaps be called Love of the Nation, or Kindness. All his life, he has detested action most of all. That he has, on occasion, acted, if quite without distinction and unnoticed by all but a few, that has been the great sacrifice of his life. No wonder he has begun to glow.

Are they done? May he now expect to remain undisturbed for the rest of the night? A bracing green smell tells him that he has been rubbed all over with some unction, perhaps to speed the mysterious processes. But what of the spluttering sip of lime-water? He has no memory of it, nor can he feel the dull weight of any intravenous tube that might else be replenishing his vital fluids. Is he then, already, past these earthly needs? Has a corner been turned, a bridge crossed, or some such metaphor? It seems unlikely, for there is an itch at the side of his hugely swollen belly that, but for the vows he took so long ago, he should very much like to scratch. This too shall pass, he knows from long experience. Itch, itch, not my itch: is that not what an old monk, when he was still a child, told him he must say to free himself from earthly concerns?

For many years that is what he tried to say to himself, whenever the need arose. Pain, pain, not my pain. Rage, rage, not my rage. And so forth. It was fully in keeping with the ancient scriptures, and he approved of the strategy from that standpoint alone. It had about it the ring of wisdom, and it took him many arduous years to recognize it for the great foolishness that it was.

He was on that fateful day, if he is not mistaken, resting under a mighty Banyan tree, in the region where he then occupied a position of some consequence. And as he stretched his legs, which were then still shapely, and cooled his feet, which he was then still able to see, in a pool of crystal-clear water, there appeared before his eyes the old monk again, in his washed-out robes, carrying one end over his arm in the approved fashion. Or at least it was an old monk very like the one who had first instructed him in the art of meditation; they are all much of a muchness, with their bald heads and baffled expressions. And the old monk spoke, in the agonizingly slow manner of such worthies, which the supreme councillor himself was to adopt later in life, as if he had all the time in the world.

'Hail and blessings,' said the monk, slowly.

35

''sings,' said the future supreme councillor.

'Remember,' said the old monk, looking out at the humming sun-haze of the clearing before them, 'remember the Way, and you shall never be lost.'

'Yes, well,' said the future supreme councillor. 'On the matter in hand, however, we cannot have any more of these encroachments, where would we be if everyone-'

'*Everyone*?' said the old monk, a smile of deep knowledge or infinite stupidity about his lips.

'No,' said the supreme councillor, 'not everyone. I see you are a literal-minded fellow. But a significant enough portion of the populace to render government efforts —'

The monk studied him with his baffled eyes. 'Is that what truly concerns you?'

'Concerns, concerns, not my concerns,' said the supreme councillor. 'On the other hand, they are the concerns I have been tasked with doing something about, by putting an end where possible to this slash-and-burn business, because it is deemed a significant threat to the national forest.'

'These are good people,' said the old monk sadly, shaking his head and looking out again at the clearing, with the handful of poor thatched hovels, and the charred husks on the ground.

'Individually, that is as may be, but collectively they are a menace. Individually, also,' said the supreme councillor, warming to his theme and lifting his feet with a splash from the crystalline pool, 'I have no doubt that despite their — ah — straitened circumstances they are faithful donors to the place of worship, whereas collectively they are a drain on the national coffers, requiring a great many man hours and personnel to be wasted — *a great many* — on stopping their nonsense, to say nothing of the significant international pressure that is being brought to bear. And since we are talking frankly here, you and I, in the simple language of the people, which for a man of your education incidentally strikes me as wholly bogus, let me add that had you given a second's thought to their welfare, you could very well have told them, from your position of undoubted authority, that there was no future in these methods, and that were they, instead of planting this frankly illegal cash crop and then abandoning the sorry patch to slash and burn a new clearing, to stay instead where they were and seek to establish through crop rotation or some such technique a self-sufficient market garden, for instance, while replenishing the surrounding forest as far as they were able, the authorities might well—'

'*Not* your concerns?' said the old monk, slyly.

And to the ears of the supreme councillor, in his fury, the hum of the insects, the cackle of the birds, the shriek of the monkeys swelled to a great roar; the sun shot a thousand daggers down through the sheltering leaves; and a great wave of stench rose from the ground, carrying notes of grass and shit and burnt wood and rotting animal carcasses, and washed all at once over him. Yes, it was as though nature itself were about to burst out of itself and reveal itself to him in all its stark boundless insanity. Oh yes, my concerns: mine. You come here, with your robes and your platitudes, your piffle about the Way, and all you are really doing is playing your vested role, as the humble spokesman of these humble people, who are significant donors, from their paltry earnings, to your well-appointed place of worship. And I am on to you, and yet I find, now I think about it, that I wholly approve. Those are rightly your concerns. These are rightly mine.

And the roar abated, and the clearing lay still and empty in the sun. And the monk was just an old man who did what he could by his lights, which were dimming: in his old trodden-down sandals, with his leathery mottled skin and his cloudy old eyes. He put in a word because he felt he must. Oh, it was something like enlightenment, when the supreme councillor saw the old wisdom for the foolishness that it was, and first understood—there at the edge of the clearing, under the great Banyan which, now he thinks about it, was probably an umbrella or sea almond tree, they are more common in such locations, sitting on a rickety bamboo bench with his feet still wet from a plastic bowl of water—it was with a great clear surge of happiness that he understood. They were all his: all itches were his, and all scratches, all joys, all pains, and all earthly concerns, his.

Padding back from the bathhouse, her hair in a queenly towel and her sponge bag pressed high against her chest, she finds—No, what now? It appears they are not nearly done. These, now, are not the attendants, whose smell he knows by heart, but rather his aides. These also he knows by their smell, for they are as powdered and perfumed a bunch of toadies as ever lived. The toad's toadies, perfectly suited to their task, of aiding and abetting him. Yet it would be rash to judge them by their appearance, or even by their musty floral smell—of day-old frangipani, if his nose is at all to be trusted—for though he has no recollection of choosing them, nor any idea how he came by them, he has found them unfailingly faithful in the handling of his worldly affairs. These men, thinks the supreme councillor, subduing with ease his irritation, cushion me well against the incessant demands of the world, and whichever way they choose to go about it is welcome to me.

And now they approach, their posture suitably humble, in a mysterious order of seniority known only to them, their voices suitably soft, and address their concerns, by way of the senior-most among them. It is only proper that the supreme councillor should lend an ear.

It is a great pink pendulous flap, his ear, with long golden hairs sprouting freely from the whorls and elevations, and into it the senior-most aide, crouching, delivers the burden of their song. He begins by sketching for the supreme councillor the layout, as it were, of the battlefield. His breath has a minty freshness. The aides have long intuited his concerns about the current administration, led by a vicious little man it amuses him to think of as the Leader, who after more than a year and a half in office shows no sign of relinquishing the post, neither through incompetence nor because a more appealing rival has arisen from the ranks.

'It is at such times,' says the senior-most aide, permitting himself a noiseless titter, 'that certain signs are observed in nature. The birds show unusual patterns of migration. The fruit trees are afflicted with blights. The pigs refuse to eat. And large numbers of squashed lizards litter the arterial roads, caught in what appears to be a frantic effort to head for the hills, or some such sanctuary. This can be attributed to some kind of stoppage in the air flow, an accumulation of pressure in the lowlands, which left unremedied may well—'

It is not, thinks the supreme councillor, that the pigs are refusing to eat, it is that they are being kept away from the feeding troughs for too long. Still, let that pass; otherwise he fully agrees with the analysis, and indeed has a feeling that he delivered much the same speech to his aides at some earlier time, and that they are merely quoting his words back at him, by way of throat-clearing.

To the point then, he thinks, to the point! Because at times like this, also, Time itself behaves in strange ways, becomes bent out of shape, squished in some places, ballooning in others, so that there is at once too much of it and none at all, even for a creature like him, who has all the time in the world.

It is unclear whether this urgency communicates itself to

---

the senior-most aide.

'It would at any rate seem,' he resumes, 'that events have been set in train which, with delicate and judicious handling—'

While some believe me to be the oldest living creature in this country, thinks the supreme councillor, including sea turtles, I am not yet so senile that I have forgotten the gist of our last consultation. We know that there appears to be glinting, in the uniform black of the current administration, One—the supreme councillor, who knows everything, knows of him but has had little occasion to study him closely—who may, with judicious and delicate handling, provide some sort of vent or valve whereby the current blockage may be relieved. This we know. It is only in the run of day-to-day business that you are, *qua* your appointed role, ahead of me.

'Quite so,' says the senior-most aide. 'We have, in short, had a communication from the man in question, or rather his people, further to their inquiry whether your Excellency would, given certain conditions—'

Yes.

'—in a so-called exclusive venue of their choosing that will no doubt, by the lights of such people—' He permits himself another soundless titter. 'In short, to preside at his daughter's wedding—'

Yes, yes.

'—which would, as previously discussed, require your Excellency to appear, so to speak, personally. But given the growing urgency of the situation—'

Quite.

'In short, we have now received—ah—a financial offer from the man in question that does not seem entirely negligible, and would go some way—'

The world sees him, as it were, through the powdered and perfumed, the softly-spoken, the pink-tied and clean-shirted and self-effacing, the ever-shifting front, of his aides; they are, yes, above all like the billowing curtains that surround his recumbent form. So long as they surround the supreme councillor, no harm can come to him; he cannot be punched, or knifed, or shot, for his recumbent form can barely be made out through their ever-shifting, powdered, perfumed flounce. It would take such a barrage of artillery to lay waste to him, such a fleet of helicopter gunships, as no one in this nation is yet able to muster, nor will be, for a century or two to come. They would permit no requests to disturb his ease unless they had good reason to suppose that it could bring great benefit to the nation.

Thanks, therefore, are due to his aides, and careful thought to the proposal.

5.

The minister leaves the back way. The underground car park is like a vat of hot petrol-flavoured soup. For a moment he feels dizzy and gasps like a fish, but already the unmarked minivan pulls up. He waves a flunkey aside, slides the door open and heaves himself in. The vehicle has its own stink, of glue and rotten apples, but the dead air is ice-cold and, sinking into the cream vinyl upholstery, he soon breathes more easily. The flunkey slides the door shut with a hollow thunk; they are on their way. This is a driver he trusts, not least because he pays him out of his own pocket.

Soon they are crossing the river, swollen and listless after the rain. From the bridge, the minister looks down at the brown water. Boats and barges of all sizes throng the water, heading in five directions, godowns to one side, tall hotels to the other, and in the shadow of the bridge, fringed by its own hedge of water hyacinth and rubbish, a slum, its flimsy walkways of grey wooden planks just visible from here.

This is an error both progressives and reactionaries make, to assume that the new will cleanly replace the old; that once we can fly we will cease to float. Here is proof to the contrary. This river is no beauty, but she remains a vital thoroughfare, as lively or more so than in feudal times, and megatons of cargo, legal and illegal, make their way into the port every day. Why, at the pier, as they speed towards the other bank, he can see the river buses sitting nose-to-tail in a regular traffic jam.

A river, there is another metaphor for the great task. Damming and dredging, ensuring traffic flow, protecting cargo. In certain lights everything is like everything: a house, like a bird, may have wings. Best perhaps not to push these things too far.

They turn left into the great road that runs along it, worse now for being wet under a thick grey-white lid of sky, and looking like a patchwork of rags sown together with old wire. Surfaces, thinks the minister, these are all we have. His memories of the old university town, now, are of the silent solidity of the structures there, their calm undeniable weight, and revenants of a dead civilisation frantically scuttling among them like roaches stirred from under a mossy stone. Here, all is deniable. No two square feet are the same, and even where the road for a few hundred metres runs perfectly straight there are no lines of sight. The eye has nowhere to rest, because no surface can claim any value over any other. The effect is fretful sameness. Plane, grid, corrugation, glaze, mesh. Concrete, tarmac, tarpaulin, brick, plaster, iron, steel, tin, rubber, fibreglass, glass. Particleboard; thermoplastic polymer. The eternal smears of damp and discoloration. Dirt, soot, rot, dust, rust— He leans back against the cream vinyl and for a moment shuts his eyes.

Thick-tongued and greasy-eyed, he comes to. They are turning off the main road. A deep breath. The way his mother would stand outside the storehouse at nightfall, rhythmically swinging her arms. The way the clawed hands would barely rise above waist height on the upward swing, towards the end. And yet she never ceased to believe in the efficacy of exercise, perhaps because it was a rational and active article of faith, an impatient stand taken against the gathering night. He stretches

43

his limbs.

To him, old age announces itself in a dull grinding pain in the knees, when the air conditioning is as ice-cold as this. Mentally, however, he is at the height of his powers. He barks at the driver to turn the air conditioning down. Almost immediately the soupy warmth starts creeping up from under his feet. They have slowed to a crawl in the narrow street, hobbling over homemade speed bumps among the jerry-built apartments, in their cheerful seaside colours, salmon pink or baby blue. Surfaces, yes, that was his train of thought: an infinity of surfaces, and no depth at all.

Smoke rises in torn sheets from the food stalls. Mangy dogs sleep by the roadside. Every other shop is a laundry or hairdresser's, handwritten signs spelling out prices, curling sun-bleached photographs showcasing styles. The chicken, that seems the predominant hairstyle now among the male youth. In his day, what was it? The mop top?

The Leader's son, for one, is a spectacular chicken; the spiky coxcomb above contrasts starkly with the weak round chin. The minister's own children, he supposes, plumb for more sedate fashions. Children still, and living essentially a life of distractions, they are already full members of the establishment, and in their way as old before their time as he was at their age. He was eager then to get on. It is only now that he is drawn to youth.

The minivan turns another corner, into a quieter street. The houses here are more solidly built, painted dull grey or white, and tired green foliage shields them from full view. As they pull into the car park of a nondescript apartment building, the minister takes his phone out of his pocket and dials a number. He lets it ring three times and hangs up. They wait. A security guard glances furtively at the van's tinted windows. Water drips onto the concrete from an overhead duct. Then the lift doors open and a young woman steps out, her long glossy hair still wet from the shower. She trips over to the van on high sandals, while the driver jumps out and slides the door open for her. She pulls herself in with some effort, ignoring the driver's solicitous arm.

'*Ooooiih*,' she exclaims as she throws herself back into the seat, as if she had just had to meet an extortionate demand.

'What is it?' snaps the minister.

'No,' she says. 'Nothing. These people—'

'Never mind,' he says and lightly pats her thigh.

'Oh, you do not know,' she says. 'You do not know.'

'Do not want to,' he snorts.

She stares straight ahead, reluctant to pass to the next stage of the ritual just yet. Then she laughs, turns to him, pulls up her knees and looks intently at his face. 'So where are you taking me?'

'Lunch,' he says.

'Good.'

'You are hungry?'

She laughs. 'I am always hungry.'

'It is true.'

'You always take me to lunch.'

'It is true.'

'Today I want to eat crab.'

'Crab, shrimp—'

'Crab, shrimp, mussel, lobster, clam—'

'Fish.' The minister is not really paying attention.

'*Seafood*.' She uses the foreign word.

'Ah.'

They have regained the main road and speed further along it. A stretch of hardware stores, warehouses and home improvement suppliers, the head offices of medium-sized enterprises producing chemicals, vegetable oil, animal fodder, ball bearings. Always wholesale and retail both, and profitable for the diligent families who run them. Motorcycle messengers weave in and out of the traffic, delivering urgent documents, orders in triplicate, invoices, letters of credit— No, he has no idea what it is they deliver, these armies of stick-thin little men, in their shiny black ironed-out windcheaters, with the company logos emblazoned above the heart. One comes to a halt next to them at the traffic light and stares blindly into the van. The young woman pulls a face at him, unseen.

'I hate,' she says.

'I know,' says the minister.

It is a recurrent theme, her hatred of the men of her own class and race, whom she considers rapists, gamblers, idiots and sponging brutes. No doubt she is right, by and large. He has not inquired into the reasons for her assessment but contents himself with the surmise that she has been burnt. Yet he is also convinced that she would sell him out faster than you can blink for the first pretty boy who spoke to her of love and constancy. From under his chicken hair. He snuffles.

'What is it?'

'No, no—'

'Tell.'

'They came to see me today.'

'Who came?'

'Petitioners.'

'What did they want? Money?'

He snuffles. 'On the contrary. They wanted to express their support.'

'For?'

'Me. In case I should challenge for the leadership.'

'And will you?'

'No.'

She looks at him. 'You are going to be the leader?'

'No.'

She whoops and claps. 'You are: you are going to be the leader.' She makes a show of raising her hands and bowing in supplication, in the direction of his stiff knees. 'My leader, o my leader, please help the poor.'

He snuffles. 'Enough of that.'

She contemplates him for a moment. 'Then when you become the leader, I can have a bigger apartment.'

'If I ever become the leader? Good. You shall have a bigger apartment.'

'On the other side of the river.'

'Yes, yes.'

'Near department stores.'

'Naturally.'

'But first,' she says, 'we eat.'

He performs vigorously. Keeping up his regime of ancient preparations and regular exercise, and having eaten three of the enormous oysters they served at the restaurant, with roast onion, chilli sauce, curry paste and lime, he exhibited the stamina of a much younger man.

Zinc: there can of course be no question of any measurable effect in the immediate aftermath of eating a mollusc. The boost is psychological, of that he is certain. In his student days, he came across information, quite outside his field of criminal law but remembered until now, that in certain South Sea islands the men expect to ejaculate twice a day well into old age, and therefore they do. He knew that in that fact a great truth was expressed, and vowed then that his expectations should always ride a fraction ahead of what common sense suggested were the possibilities; not too far to create a yawning gap of frustration, but far enough to lure him ever onwards and upwards. He has remained faithful to that resolve.

The girl lies catlike now, her eyes closed, all but purring, curled against his supine form. In his right hand, the second cigarette of the day. The smoke billows almost to the ceiling before it is suddenly snatched away, as if by sleight of hand, in the draft from the air conditioner. The thinnest of wood veneer covers a great many surfaces in this room, peeling here and there where it has been unable to withstand the constant flip-flop of temperatures, from chill to tropical damp. The sheet that covers him to the chest smells of bleach. He has not used this motel before, but they are much of a muchness. Each time, by contrast, he is struck afresh by the springy firmness of the girl's flesh, the two dimples on either side of the spine, the way she seems fully to inhabit her skin, even down to her buttocks, to which in the heat of intercourse she likes to administer an occasional ringing slap to make them wobble. This he considers an endearing as well as arousing detail.

Such abandon was unheard-of among the women of his own generation, or even five years ago, when modesty was still considered highly erotic, and a simpering primness could often be observed especially where it stood in inverse proportion to a woman's sexual continence. They begged for all lights to be extinguished, and pretended no matter how often they found themselves in the predicament that this was the very first time they had let themselves go, to the extent that they had. He is fortunate to have lived long enough for that grim fashion to pass. It offended among other things his practical intelligence.

His colleagues in high office tend to keep hothouse flowers, who do a great deal of soft cooing over inanimate objects and present to the world an exquisitely sculpted and quite dead face. Yet their origins are much the same as this cheerful homely girl's, among the farmlands of the upper plains. Once again he marvels at the way so many in this nation seem able to don a fresh identity whole, like a skin graft, when the circumstances conspire. The Leader has a slip of teenage girl with a finely chiselled doll's face and a steely glint in her eye. One is told she calls him *Papa*. One is told her ambitions lie in the entertainment field—as whose these days do not?—and she obsessively practices her dance routines. The minister wishes her well. It must take strong nerves to strain under that vicious, petulant man, whose resentments no doubt extend to the female of the species, and whose sleepless nights no doubt give him ample opportunity to think up unpleasantnesses to inflict on her. The foot on the head. The minister's mouth puckers with distaste.

He has been fortunate with this girl. Orgasms come easy to her and are no cause for shame. He is fond, to the extent that he is, of her uncomplicated exhibitionism, and senses a kind of innocence in her mercenary instincts. There is no side to her. It is further fortunate that she appears to take a natural pleasure in the mechanics of sex, over and above any considerations as to the person with whom she engages in it. In turn, he believes she is reasonably fond of him, taking at face value—taking as kindness—such material assistance as he is able or willing to provide, and being stirred to a simple affection by them. He reaches over for the ashtray on the wood-veneer bedside table, and she gives a grunting start.

'Sleep!' she demands, and drops off again.

Also she makes him laugh, not that he is keen to let her see it. It pleases her inordinately, to coax a reluctant smile from him.

He smokes. *Near department stores*: that is the great desideratum of life. For that clarification also he has her to thank. She has brought home the extent to which it is an as it were innocent priority for the masses. An unkind way perhaps to think of one's mistress, as *the masses*; but could it not be said that this, here, is his way of communing with them: in their undeniably particular manifestation? A salutary activity, this, not merely by way of balancing the organism and buttressing matrimonial harmony, but also in keeping him abreast of the great stream of popular sentiment, the hopes, fears, superstitions, fantasies and incessant demands by which men like him are buoyed, or drowned, as the case may be.

Time, however, is short. He grinds out his cigarette in the ashtray, lifts the girl's arm from his chest, extracts his leg from under her knee, and rises to go to the bathroom. The smell of bleach there is strong enough to bring tears to the eyes. The soap, on its wrapper, bears the brand name of what in his youth a popular disinfectant, and may for all he knows be a popular disinfectant still, its venerable aura of scrupulous cleanliness now diffused throughout a range of hygiene products. There we are, he thinks as he briskly soaps himself, image is all: a multiplicity of surfaces, and no depth.

As he rinses off the girl walks into the bathroom, on flat, padded, sleepy feet. The sight of her plump nakedness, so undefended and matter-of-fact under the strip light, stirs him again, but he has no time to spare, now, if the day's remaining tasks are to be managed efficiently. Stepping into the bathtub, the girl gives his resurgent penis an affectionate tug and takes the shower nozzle out of his hand, to hold it over her own head. He climbs out and wraps himself in a towel.

From now on he is all business. Ablutions over, they will powder their private parts, dress, and step directly into the car park and thence the van, whereupon the driver will draw the heavy green felt curtain that has protected their privacy, and their car's, from the curiosity of passers-by and drive to the main road, through the glaring afternoon haze. The girl will quickly sniff his cheek there, step out of the car and take a taxi the rest of the way, for the minister has a schedule to observe that permits of no further detours, and racing along he will cross the river again and finally with all but squealing tyres reenter the official car park, where a flunkey will be waiting by the lift to accompany him to the tall gloomy office where he reigns supreme. He will confer with his chief of staff. He will be advised by advisers. He will plot; he will plan; dry, lipless, bony, devoid of charisma, behind a massive imposing desk, under the awful portraits.

Orders will be given. Order will advance.

6.

Padding back from the bathhouse, her hair in a queenly towel and her sponge bag pressed high against her chest, she finds another woman waiting for her by the door; there is something of the heron or crane about her visitor, elongated and keen, and she starts talking immediately.

The woman grunts and, pushing her visitor aside, and busies herself with the padlock.

The visitor's tale is of someone she shares accommodation with. Then I said, and then she said. Neither the woman nor the supreme councillor pay much attention. Nor for that matter does the visitor seem greatly invested, delivering herself of it much as a bird delivers itself of its morning song, heedless of its reception, and in a tone of wry amusement that perhaps owes more to some pre-set sequence than any intrinsically amusing quality to her story. The only sign the woman gives of being aware of her visitor is in the vigour with which she now seizes a truncated broom, with a pink handle, to sweep particularly in the area the visitor currently occupies, so that an observer might mistake their steps and side-steps for a formal mating dance.

In the cramped premises this soon becomes untenable, and with a last vigorous thrust the woman sweeps the dust out of the door, latches it, undoes the towel around her head and starts to towel her hair. She does this layer by layer, her head indulgently inclined to one side, her knees slightly bent under the shapeless bathing smock and her feet turned outward as if to secure a better purchase on the deck of a pitching ship. The visitor, meanwhile, takes a seat on the mattress, looks around her, seizes from a small glass perched on a little shelf above the bed a nail file, and attends to her fingernails, which due to the exceptional thinness and length of her fingers also resemble the talons of some water fowl.

She does not once stop speaking.

For whom if not for each other, wonders the supreme councillor, do they go through these motions? They cannot be aware of his presence, which in any case is dubious even to him. He is there perhaps only in a manner of speaking, and certainly not in any palpable manifestation. Perhaps, he thinks, it is that there is comfort in these motions, in these poor hovels, and more than that: decorum, and that as long as decorum attends on our interactions, we may yet be comforted.

The comb now, for the one-hundred strokes. Had the woman not bleached her naturally black hair to a kind of tainted copper, she would not now need to look so ruefully at the split ends, the tangles that come away in the prongs. It occurs to the supreme councillor that she is being deliberately slow about it, and a slight widening of the eyes and pursing of the mouth tells him that it amuses her to keep her visitor waiting.

There can be no doubt that she has come about urgent business, despite the aimless wry wittering, and that it will have to wait in proportion to its urgency. He too finds himself entering into the spirit, mentally dawdling on the brink of some development that he is not yet ready to witness. The comb also: though bald as a coot he can feel it tugging at his own scalp, and a warm tingle tells him that the area benefits from increased blood flow. Could he, if he chose, hurry them along? Would space-time bend to his wishes? It is a moot point because he does not wish, and this is one of the places about which he has spoken where Time behaves in unexpected ways.

Just as he is about to drift from these reflections into a deeper sleep, there comes a knock on the door.

'Who?' the woman asks.

A single syllable, and the woman sighs and opens the door.

'My,' says the second visitor, looking her up and down. 'You have just got up?'

'No,' says the woman. 'I have been up for a long time.'

'Just in a mood then,' says the second visitor cheerfully, and comes in after the retreating woman. She is ample and maternal, with a generous bosom and a cheerful, pretty face that, the woman knows, make her popular with men of all ages. With women too; even she can feel herself perking up, much as she may struggle to uphold this crotchety facade.

The second visitor nods hello to the crane-like girl, who resumes her story, and finds herself a comfortable spot on the mattress. She has brought her own sponge bag, and now unzips it to take out a pair of tweezers. Lifting one arm lazily over her head, pressing her face into her shoulder, she attacks a stubble of underarm hair. Their hostess goes back to her rueful combing. For some minutes the three women sit and attend to their grooming tasks, accompanied by the flat sing-song of the first visitor's tale.

Suddenly the woman groans, crushes a tangle of hair in her fist and throws it on the floor, rises, stomps over to the shelf above the mattress, and switches on a small pink transistor radio. She turns the volume up full and returns, stomping, to her place.

'Ui.' The crane-like visitor's head comes up, keenly.

The maternal woman giggles from under her arm and pats her on the skinny knee. 'Enough already,' she says. 'Who wants to hear it?'

'Not me,' mutters their hostess.

'Up to you,' says the first visitor, and with a shrug goes back to her nails. Even at full blast the radio is capable of barely more than a kind of plasticky whisper, making a little prison for the song that struggles to rise from its core. It is a lilting, dragging song of love and chicken noodles which, it strikes the supreme councillor, has the exact same circular quality as the story it interrupted, the same banal to-and-fro without rising to any great pitch, and the words, confined as they are to the exact same register, seem to be of no greater consequence, as if the radio had merely picked up where the woman left off.

This too is an observation the supreme councillor has made before, that the popular music, and indeed all art, in this country seems wholly of a piece with what you might call the structure of the nation's consciousness. And further, he thinks, that the seamless way the acoustic background has passed from one medium to another, from live delivery to broadcast and from speech to song, without changing its essential quality, speaks to a great mysterious continuity in this nation between I and not-I, subject and object, body and spirit, and — yes, why not? — animate and inanimate, and life and death.

And while this great mysterious continuity, this profound underlying sameness of everything, must be the case everywhere, he has often pitied other nations, and especially those commonly called *advanced*, for surrounding that great mysterious underlying truth with such a thicket of flimflammery and such forbidding ramparts, both notional and physical, that it can only be glimpsed here and there by the most eagle-eyed observer, if indeed it can be glimpsed at all. Whereas in this nation the great mystery is plain for all to see, and that is what makes it, notwithstanding certain superficial material and spiritual handicaps, the greatest nation on earth.

By degrees the women have progressed to the makeup stage. A bewilderment of little zippered bags now sit, maws gaping, on the varied surfaces. They take turns to fish from them the tools of their labour: lotions and unctions, mirrors, brushes, pencils, pads and puffs. Here, too, notions seem curiously smeared from mine into not-mine, and any residual tension in the room dissolves in the pleasure they take in enhancing their features to the best possible advantage. They dab and wipe and draw and smudge, their eyes turn heavenward, their noses wrinkle, their mouths purse and pout. With a flick of the wrist, one unfolds a sheet of tissue paper, then folds it again, clamps it in her mouth and leaves on it a perfect imprint of her lips, holding it at arm's length to admire. Another, inspired, takes a sheet to correct the kohl outline in the corner of her eye, folds it over, wipes again, and examines her handiwork in the mirror.

A terrible hiss gives both visitors a start, but it is only their hostess, fiercely spraying her hair as though punishing it for her sins. You could cut the air in the hut with a knife now, so thick and heady is it with smells and chemicals. In truth all their eyes are red. If you were to come in now, you would stagger backwards from the miasma, and from the force of their theatrically painted features under the day-bright fluorescent tube. They are nearly done, but the woman, instead of putting on a going-out dress, merely pulls a bra, an outsize old t-shirt and a pair of beach shorts out of the relevant bags. She turns her back on her visitors and slips them on under and over the bathing smock.

'Ah,' she says.

The maternal woman, a great voluptuous beauty now, with smouldering eyes, calmly teases her sponge bag towards her and takes out three banknotes, which she hands to their hostess without comment. The hostess grunts and stuffs them into the holster of her phone. The crane-like woman starts wittering again, in the same lilting sing-song, but before she can settle into her narrative the hostess cuts in.

'You want or not?'

The crane-like woman shakes her head, sighs, and takes her time extracting from her own bra a single banknote that has been folded and folded and folded again to the size of a coin. The hostess whips it out of her hand, snorts at it, and adds it to the others. Without another word, intently pressing buttons on her phone, she lets herself out, slips into her rubber sandals, and shuts the door behind her with a thump that sets the whole old hut a-tremble.

7.

A slum, the supreme councillor notes approvingly, is the quietest place on Earth. If you stood outside now, in the enveloping dark, you would have to prick up your ears to hear the snick of their lighters, the gurgle of the water behind their teeth, the quickening murmur of their conversation, the whispering radio. There would be slow sloshing perhaps from the canal, and bullfrogs honking their one sad mechanical note, and in the distance the hum of traffic, ebbing and swelling on the great elevated road that runs across the city like a bold aquifer over a desert waste. Someone is always coughing, and the slap of water on porcelain speaks of discreet ablutions, of guarded privacies. Voices barely rise above a mutter, except when an infant is briefly roused from its slumber and soon put down again. Now and again a motorcycle clanks and snarls into life and fades away.

But then a muffled thunk-*thump* along the rotten boards of the walkway. Coming this way, breathing heavily, thunk-*thump*ing in a great hobbled hurry towards the old hut. A stumble, a strangled cry, and then a fast heavy knock on the door.

Fleet fingers gather the utensils, almost too fast for the naked eye to catch. A flash of silver foil, a clatter of lighters, now you see them, now not: a last push at the loose floorboard, a last hissing blast of deodorant or hairspray, whatever comes to hand. The rolled-up towel under the door kicked out of the way, picked up seamlessly by the maternal woman, unrolled, as if she had been drying her hands on it all along. A last quick look around.

'Who?'

'Open up.'

She fumbles frantically with the latch and rips the door wide open. And there he stands, the son.

But how battered, how beaten down; what a sorry figure in the harsh light from the single fluorescent tube. The thin arms hanging limply down his sides, the swaddled leg, the stupid grey mummy bandage around the head, from underneath which a purple eye casts a look of doglike submission at his mother.

'*Aaaaaaiii!*' She tears from the nail nearest the door a violent-green handbag, and sets about his bandaged head with such fury that she must surely do all the damage all over again. '*Ai, ai ai ai!*'

For long seconds he stands, shielding his head against her fury. The other women sit stunned. Then, as if he feels he has now been given his due, he ducks in slow motion and squats, gorilla-fashion, sumo-fashion, and clumsily tries to get a grip on the furious woman's hard wiry waist.

'Mother,' he mutters thickly. 'Mother.' Then more firmly, 'mother!' swinging further out with the gangly arms until he gets some purchase at last on her waist through the billowing t-shirt, wrestling her now. Her arms are high up over her head now, so she can still get a clear hit at the stupid bandaged head, though the force of the blows is greatly diminished at this awkward angle and only raises little puffs of exposed hair. Their breath comes hard, and she is still shrieking, but more raggedly now.

'Mother!' He is laughing now, trying to wrestle her into the hut and towards the bed, where the crane-like woman has jumped up to make room for them. And through her fury his mother, too, starts to laugh, raggedly, angrily, but laugh all the same.

The maternal woman gently shuts the door. 'Shhh,' she

says.

They cannot deny the force of that argument, here in the quiet slum, and the mother, still breathing hard, tries as it were to stuff herself back into the box. This takes some doing, but by and by the bulk of her fury is tucked out of sight, and though she is still scowling she does not pose an immediate threat to the life and limb of others.

Cooing and clucking, the other two women coax the youth's story out of him, each in their own style—the maternal woman gently amused, the crane-like one perky and keen.

He tells it reluctantly and in a croaking voice barely used to its lower registers. His expression is both slack and strained. How old can he be? Sixteen, perhaps, seventeen; maturity comes late to this nation, and according to its detractors never comes at all. As if the great aim of existence—thinks the supreme councillor, who has had lifetime of dealings with officials from overseas—were to transmute as soon as possible after graduation into a sack of rocks sewn into an armour-plated suit, animated, if that is the word, by a sort of primitive arrangement of cogs and wheels, clanking along, puffs of blackish exhaust emerging from the posterior. Well, that was his first impression of the foreigners, that and their penetrating smell of cheese. But he has since come to understand that the grown-up races, too, yearn in the fat soft centre of their armoured heads for ease and grace, for song, and laughter, and love. Oh, give them a bit of this and that and they all but turn into a quivering jelly before your eyes.

The son, at any rate, is having his story pulled out of him by his mother's visitors, with coos and clucks. He is gauche and sullen, and terrified by the attention of these magnificently painted and perfumed creatures, their glistening lips, their lush aura of sin, but tickled also, that it is over him they should be clucking and cooing and giggling. Yes, the more he tells it, the more he comes to life; uncouth around the edges, unsteady of voice and wincing occasionally at the leaden patches of pain all over his body, but back to life he comes.

The story—well, it is what the supreme councillor has so often heard bemoaned as a *social problem*. What can you say about it? That on certain weekend nights, perhaps in relation to the phases of the moon or some other mysterious pattern, the lads in their hundreds gather on the outer ring roads, where thanks to certain planning irregularities they have the ten-lane highway more or less to themselves— And how fortuitous, the supreme councillor interrupts himself, that these irregularities, so called, should yet result in a space where these young people may express their overflowing animal spirits. So often the forces of life conspire in mysterious ways to turn a small wrong into a greater right, and what seems a senseless wasteland to the untutored eye reveals on certain nights its hidden riches—

The lads in their hundreds, at any rate, gather there in the small hours, in a great roaring cacophony of doctored and slimlined scooters, in blazing clusters of headlights, and amid great thumping music from sound systems mounted on bikes and pickup trucks.

Meanwhile their girlfriends, dolled up to the nines, mere slips of stretchy textile clinging to this or that part of their anatomy, with glossy hair and glamorous shoes on their bare feet, in approximate sizes, screech and chatter as they line up on the overpasses, shouting out taunts and mocking encouragement, promising fleshly rewards, all as excited as a cage full of yelping puppies— And oh, such love has gone into the machines, all superfluous bulges stripped away and replaced with flat shiny aluminium covers, the suspension coils all the colours of the rainbow, shafts raised, seats lowered, exhaust pipes gleaming marvels of ingenuity. How cheerfully they embrace their prescribed roles, the boys all drive and thrust, the girls all soft glistening promise. You cannot hear yourself think and you would not want to—not that much thought ever entered these people's heads at the best of times, and certainly not now, except of sex and light and glory.

And then they line up, and despite the terrific noise a great hush seems to fall over the congregation, a long tense noisy silence. Then with a flat crack someone fires a gun—they all have guns—and they are off. Ah, the great rushing speed, the skill and control that rule the vast scrum as it churns and thunders towards the distant finish line. To survive the five-hundred metres alone is glory, though perhaps the greater glory still is to die here, a hero, on this stretch of unwanted infrastructure, with the siren wailing you to your rest. The songs are written, the lines rehearsed: how the girl, ferried there on a bystander's scooter, will drop from a sort of tangle on the back of it, and throw herself on the body, and weep, supported and comforted by the best of friends, yet inconsolable sometimes for whole weeks on end.

But then, also, the hair's-breadth escapes, the beautiful long skidding arcs, the near-harmless tumble. And for the rest, the elation of having come through, and got away too, in the aftermath, from the clumsy but powerful old bikes of the police, down the side streets and back ways, like giving an angry bull elephant a run for his money.

And then, having shaken them off, whooping already with wild triumph on the muddy dirt track behind some bone-white silent apartment blocks, to hit a stone, and slide sideways, and skitter along on the soft ground, and come to rest *thwack* against a half-built garden wall, supine among the discarded tires—

At this point in the tale the mother's two friends are weeping with laughter, but the mother says only: 'And the bike?'

He sobers abruptly, and looks down at his bandaged hand,

his stick-thin abraded arms.

'Totalled.'

And she is up again. '*Aaaaaiiii*', and, seizing a sponge bag, hers or someone else's, sets about his thick mummy-head again, with true venom this time, because the bike is not paid for, and he will need another, how else is he to get around? And the other two women have to grab her and clamp hands over her mouth and prize her off the boy and hold her down, and keep her fast while she rocks and rocks herself and wails and gasps with the terrible grief of it all.

Well, her makeup is ruined after that, to say nothing of the hair. Even barring these unforeseen developments the makeup was always going to need touching up if it was applied before the drugs had been enjoyed. It might be concluded, thinks the supreme councillor, that the two ceremonies, of the application of the makeup and the inhaling of the drugs, are as yet poorly integrated with one another, or else that they are becoming as it were intertwined and are merging, by gradual adjustments as yet incomplete, into a single evening ritual—if 'evening' is the right word to describe this already late hour, which is nonetheless early, given how recently the participants have got up. These things, then, will right themselves by and by.

Once the mother has sufficiently calmed down, the other two women drift away to get dressed for the night. The crane-like woman witters on the way out, doling out wry remarks not only to mother and son but as though she were greeting a phalanx of fans at the stage exit. The maternal woman in the end forcefully pulls her out of the door, to leave the other two in peace. They sit for a moment in separate glum silence, then the mother speaks.

'So?' Her voice is rough from shrieking.

He waits, then the words come out as though leaking from a cracked egg. 'I am sorry.'

'Yes.'

A rattle in the distance tells her that her two visitors have arrived in their own huts.

'Where will we find the money?' she starts again.

'I can work.'

She lets time pass but does not sneer. 'Where?'

He shrugs.

'You will have to sell.'

He stares, then perks up. 'Do you think?'

'What else?'

'Motorcycle taxi.'

'Well, yes—'

Already he is quite cheerful again and starts to get up. 'Tomorrow I ask.'

'And the hospital?'

'The girl—' the boy says. 'Then she threw me out.'

The mother releases air through the nose, but when she casts a quick sideways glance at him, he catches her eye, and they both start to laugh. She takes a couple of banknotes out of her purse and shoves them at him. 'Ah.'

'Thank you,' he makes to raise his hands in gratitude but she raises her hand as if to strike him again.

'Out.'

On his way out he turns around once more, eyes brimming with sincerity. 'Tomorrow,' he says, but her face is bent over her sponge bag as she prepares to fix the damage.

She takes out a mirror and checks. The eyes like a tragic mask's, tracks of kohl running down her cheeks. The boil an angry red beacon. The lipstick leaching into the foundation. Blusher everywhere. Still, she is fired up now, and the blood runs hot and fast through her veins; a few swift firm wipes with an alcohol-soaked cotton wad clear up the devastation, and though her hands are trembling her touch is deft and sure. Within a few minutes she has repaired what took her scores the first time, fury standing in for patient artistry. The hair now, with punishing strokes of the brush—No. She gathers it up in a velvet-sleeved rubber band with three strokes from each hand and, from one of the countless nails on her wall, takes a baseball hat, a gift from a foreign admirer, puts it on, threads the ponytail through the adjustable clasp at the back, and is ready for the clothes. A sporting look: hotpants, a t-shirt with a large square-lettered number, footlets, and the running shoes. Only once, for a tangled instant with the second bow, does she permit herself an exclamation—oi!—and then she is done. A final blast of cologne paints an ampersat on her upper body; bag, light, lock. On her way across the first bouncing planks she dials a number on her phone, to say she can wait no longer.

Most of the Cabinet are at golf now, where it is said all the important decisions are made. The minister has no opinion on the matter, nor does he begrudge them their leisure. With most of the Cabinet, the permanent secretary is vastly better placed to do the job, and a minister's presence in the office only diverts manpower and resources from the tasks in hand and disturbs, with its ripples, the smooth running of the country. Not so here. His presence here has a galvanizing effect, for one thing, and for another he likes to spend the hot white afternoons out of the glare, amid the industrious hum of the old air conditioners, feeling the pulse of toil throb all around him. Perhaps after all he is in his true element here, at the brain or nerve centre of a vast organism whose tentacles reach into every corner of the nation.

The Leader would not think so. The Leader has a great notion that the centre is wherever he chooses to go. He often golfs in full view of the national press, trailed about the green by a gaggle of sweating reporters, holding incessantly forth. And when he came to the minister with his proposal, he summoned him to the golf course he favoured at the time. How long ago now? Two-and-a-half years, a dry warm winter day. They have come far since then.

The summons was no surprise, feelers having for some time been put out. Yet being summoned into anyone's presence triggers apprehension; even if it is understood what the discussion will be about, and even if the person into whose presence one is being summoned is at that time neither in a position of authority over one nor greatly to be feared for other reasons. The minister would like to think he obeyed it out of curiosity alone, but there is no denying that on the drive to the airport, where the golf course nestled between two runways, his mouth was drier than usual, his nerve ends tingled, and his scrotum sat more snugly in the fork of his legs than it normally would with a man of his age.

On arrival at the club house he was met by a nervous man in an outsize crested blazer, who was perhaps the manager or in some way attached to the new Party machine, and who told him that the Leader was already waiting—he all but added, *impatiently*—at the first tee-box, and would the future minister kindly follow him. His clubs were heaved into the back of the cart, which presently trundled off across the grass. The blazered fellow's slightly tremulous hands on the wheel communicated their unsteadiness to the minister's innards. The cart purred and wobbled, and the hazy air shimmered in a way that, you could almost believe, was a function of the distant high keening of the jet engines. They gained a little ridge, they rounded a tree, and there, at the tee-box, was the Leader. A caddy stood at attention and a little back, on slightly higher ground, two generic heavies watched over the scene. They might have been cut from plywood and propped there, so impassively did they look on as the Leader, centre picture, practiced his swing. Oh yes, it had been carefully set up.

He was a peculiar sight, the Leader, dressed in a grey polo shirt and black slacks and wearing not only a tall black baseball hat but also a pair of black plastic mirrored shades that looked as though they had come from a street stall but probably cost more than he had ever legally earned during a month in the force. The notion of leisure was thus given a strangely official or businesslike cast, the cheerfully clashing clothes of the sport reduced to monochrome, subordinated to the greater will of a man who could not quite decide whether he operated darkly within or without the legal spectrum, and was perhaps content to leave the ambiguity unresolved.

They approached, but it was only when the flunkey stopped the cart that the Leader looked up from his exercises and pretended to notice them for the first time.

'Ah,' he said, and smiled.

The minister felt a brief but powerful stab of revulsion. The Leader is cursed with a great cuboid head on whose front-facing side a set of babyish features sit bunched, a large pair of hooded slow baby eyes behind the shades, and under the little nose a mouth like a bisected worm. It smiled now, coyly, while the head performed a mincing little dip, and the fluttering eyes became just visible over the rim of the shades. Yes, it was as though the future minister had just put a slightly outrageous proposal to him, which the Leader was nonetheless understood to be considering, in a spirit of ghastly playfulness.

The moment passed, then both had their hands up and their heads down in greeting.

'Ah.'

And yet, in the course of their game, he found himself, not perhaps warming to the Leader, but thawing. It was so evident to both of them how much they disliked each other; they were so careful to avoid each other's eyes; the joviality of their talk was so exquisitely strained; that their mutual discomfort provided a kind of bond as they tramped side by side across the hard dry grass. The minister further appreciated, he thinks now, that the Leader made no further attempt, after the little staged scene on arrival, to lord it over him. Indeed, the unease that came off him suggested that the Leader, too, had been nervous about the encounter, and remained nervous still. He has never acquired the ease that comes with enormous wealth, and takes so little for granted.

Against all expectations the Leader was good at golf. He had clearly worked diligently at his game, and he had what for want of a better word must be called an elegant swing. There was one point when he stood, having carefully chosen a five-iron, silhouetted on a little mound in his absurd hat, with a toy-like silvery passenger jet suspended motionless behind him in the hazy yellow sky; and the arms came up, the long torso turned, the leg lifted daintily on tip-toe, and he swung and hit the sweet spot—*chock*—and the minister suddenly found himself filled with admiration. And he thought, what an elegant swing!

He called out the ceremonial 'good shot!' with real conviction, and the Leader's babyish old-maid's face came once again horribly into its own. The head dipped, the eyes fluttered up, and a pleased little smile stole across the wormy sphincter of a mouth as though it was quite beyond his control.

The minister too, though not naturally gifted, has worked hard at his game and prides himself on a certain competence, and that day he thought he recognized in the Leader, despite their mutual dislike, a kindred soul, in that regard. And he sensed that the Leader recognized the same in him. So that on that hazy golf course, in the sticky heat, amid the keening of the jet engines and the Leader's incessant jabbering, the minister-to-be came under the impression that between him and the Leader an incongruous bond of respect was forged, whose subject was not so much their political acumen, which they took for granted in one another, but their skill—their hard-won but undeniable skill—at the game of golf.

That was how it was settled, and in due time, election won by a landslide, the formal offer of the Cabinet post came, and he accepted it. Once more he wore uniform, for the swearing-in. For the most part they were as dissolute a rabble as the last lot—the bulging bellies, the dyed hair, the thug faces—except two or three who had been picked for competence alone. Finance looked sourly down his long nose, under a bouffant of blow-dried hair that rivalled the wives' at the back. Transport seemed to have anointed himself from top to toe in engine lubricant. Agriculture and Fisheries had but lately emerged from the plough. Culture—ah, Culture: he has since found her an ally in certain aspects of his great task, but only perhaps because he alone among his colleagues has not deigned to snicker at the poor cow, whose sole reading all her life has been the society magazines and certain tracts, ghost-written, by a withered monk from the lower plains who is driven about in an enormous luxury car. Sport he took an immediate liking to, a bland young fellow with a keen eye, if you caught it, and twenty years younger than the rest, who stood perfectly still while the rest of them shifted their weight from leg to leg in respectful boredom as the ceremony bumbled along.

The Leader himself seemed on the verge of hugging himself with glee, for the hour or so that it took. And when they were done bowing and scraping, and the reverent expressions slowly fell from their faces the way darkness fades at dawn, and they had taken the family photograph on the august steps, the Leader announced to the national press, in thin, high, giddy tones, that their work was to start *immediately*. That was how they first found out and—now the minister thinks about it—their first taste of the style in which the Leader proposed henceforth to govern the nation.

Having it sprung on you like that, before the TV cameras, what were you to do? The minister exchanged a bland look with Sport, and made his way to the official car, for the first of the Cabinet meetings which have since become such a notorious ordeal for the Leader's stable. The wives took it hardest of all, standing all lost in the forecourt with their hard hair and their intricate web of animosities, and none but each other to express their indignation to.

Only Foreign Affairs was not to be taken thus by surprise: he simply slunk down an alley along the way and was gone. He is in many ways exactly like an old cat, Foreign Affairs, blessed with a sixth and seventh sense for the vicissitudes of office, never to be found when you want him but always, when you have just given up on him, materialising in a corner of the room: serene, mildly distracted, and looking as if he had been there all along. Oh, Foreign Affairs is a smoother operator than all the rest of them together, the minister readily concedes, but for that reason useless, too, in any post but the one he holds. His entire political acumen lies in the diplomatic sphere, and all his diplomacy is avoidance.

And yet Foreign Affairs is a devoted family man and spent the first coalition crisis—or so it is said—in a convoy, chasing a girl for whom his son had conceived a passion down the highway to a seaside resort, where her own family had thought to spirit her out of the son's immediate reach. Well, they caught up by and by, and the whole thing came to a head at a rest stop near the deep-sea port, and once the obligatory pleas had been delivered, and the obligatory tears shed, they brought out the hampers and made a picnic of it. Now the girl, still pure as far as that goes, studies for her master's degree abroad, and the son has found happiness with another.

All vital matters in this country are conducted in close proximity to farce. And yet blood is spilt, and men die, and hearts are broken: hence order, the vital importance of. The minister, unobserved here in his tall cool office, allows himself a snuffle of satisfaction, at the elegant turn his thoughts have taken.

The day of the swearing-in, at any rate, the rest of them were cornered like rats, or herded like cattle, or some such metaphor, into their first Cabinet meeting—outfoxed, outmanoeuvred, stumped, and reduced to gasping and grinding their teeth as the Leader held forth, uninterrupted, for two-and-a-half hours. They still had their ceremonial uniforms on, with the gold epaulettes and the dubious decorations; and as the creases deepened around the ministerial bellies, and the stains under their arms darkened, and the shoulders rode higher around their ears—and their stomachs, moreover, rumbled, for there had been no warning to ready the snacks, and all that came in after a good long while was awful instant coffee, with the accursed powdered whitener—the Leader spoke, uninterrupted, about his goals, and his schemes, and the great things they were going to do for this nation.

The torrent of language that comes out of the man, in his thin, high, grating voice. Despite the mouth's sphincter-like appearance, the Leader lacks some essential mechanism, some sphincter or valve normally interposed between the upper layer of thought, where we think in more or less fully formed words, and the speech apparatus that makes them audible. It is a defect he appears to share with a number of despots we read about in the history books, who are reported by surviving flunkeys to have regularly talked themselves to sleep at the dinner table. The effect is not so much of an avalanche as of a landfill, where each cartload of words that pours out of his mouth is immediately buried under a fresh one, so that while no meaning in the conventional sense can be gleaned from any one sentence, the accumulation by and by shapes itself into a sort of vague but distinctive mass against the hazy sky in which his general aims, beliefs and aspirations may be surmised. Thus, too, did the terms of their agreement emerge during the game of golf.

And yet it would be quite wrong, thinks the minister now, to look in these vague shapes for truth. Rather, it is as if the Leader, finding himself unable to stopper this incessant flow of words, has instead perfected the art of lying as it were cumulatively, and piling up mounds of verbal garbage that both in their vague outline and in the locations in which they are placed give a wholly false representation of his mental landscape.

In a way the minister's own feelings for the Leader do not greatly matter; he is under the impression that no-one likes the Leader much, and that he bought every friend he ever had. If anything this has felt like an advantage in their dealings with one another, because it reduced their relationship to the level of simple transactions, and given the similarity of their backgrounds he has long felt that they both prefer simple transactions to other forms of human intercourse. The minister does not expect a rich warm human glow from his working relationships. His eye is on the goal—or if you will the swing and putt—and he understands himself above all as instrumental. Two instruments, then, working harmoniously towards the greater goal; or so he thought at the time.

9.

Perhaps it was a mistake to win the game. This occurs to the minister only now. His own vanity being invested in his acquired skill in the matter of golf, he had perhaps overlooked the Leader's craven dependency on winning in all matters. Craven dependency on winning; the paradox pleases the minister. He supposes his own vanity is invested, too, in his intellect, and he supposes further, alone here in his tall darkening office, that he feels intellectually superior to everyone in this country. This may or may not be a function of his ethnic minority status; it is also perhaps a correct assessment. Certainly the Leader, although belonging to the same ethnic minority, has no mind to speak of, and is in some respects a startlingly stupid man. One must be careful on this train of thought as it hurtles on its narrow-gauge tracks into the valley below.

Because intellect is no prerequisite, nor perhaps even a useful corollary, to leadership. The minister is aware that he tends to pronounce such words with a certain eager, spitting emphasis and avoids them in conversation. They belong to other cultures and traditions and are—like prayer or masturbation—best indulged in private. He is at any rate not a philosopher. Or by analogy with science, he is no theoretical physicist but an engineer. He dams and bridges. He applies. He is when all is said and done a man of action. But considered action, there is the difference. He is no juggernaut; he does not hurtle headlong, crushing everything in his path, nor does he on the whole veer and swerve. He steers a steady course.

Who better then—he imagines his friend the superintendent asking—to lead this nation, this veering, swerving, flailing, unruly nation, than a man who steers a steady course? Who better, once the Leader's fizz, crackle and pop is spent, to take over the reins, calm the horses, and steer the chariot of state once more on the straight path? Or to put it another way, who else? He snuffles, and hawks into the wastepaper basket.

There can be no doubt that their two vehicles, whatever their nature, are set on a collision course. Because what the Leader craves most is love, a treasure all his money has yet to unlock. Whereas the minister, who knows himself as an austere, even forbidding figure, lizardly of aspect and thin on charm, is nonetheless loved, without seeking it, by women much like his own wife. He snuffles. Mothers, protectors of property, who believe themselves under siege on all sides. Who believe disorder to be pushing at their ornate gates, ready to gobble up their children the moment they let them out. These are his core constituency. It is only just, he thinks, that he should be seen to do his best on their behalf. He has not chosen them, they have chosen him. That is something he feels the Leader cannot forgive.

A wilier politician, the minister decides, would have let the Leader win his game: by a hard-fought point or two, but win it all the same. He could have fumbled a putt at the strawy eleventh hole and nobody would be the wiser. But is it not—since we are on the question of *leadership*—the winners who win, and the losers who by and large lose? Is it not therefore in the nature of a winner that he wins, even at golf, and by the same token a fatal chink in a man's armour if he allows himself to lose, even at golf?

The question, then, is no longer whether to strike but when. For, having exposed the chink in the Leader's armour, the minister must sooner or later be crushed in some other way. That follows from the psychology. The Leader leaves no perceived slight unavenged, and while he is capable of forgetting his own words within minutes, and of denying them strenuously the next day, he nonetheless has the memory of an elephant for any perceived slight.

It is said, for example— Well, the story is a meal in itself. The Leader came by the seeds of his enormous fortune dishonestly; to this no one has any objections, even less so since the victim of his dishonesty was also a dishonest man, who had sought to subvert the laws of the land, and what is more, a foreigner. Or in another light, the victim was an entrepreneur with an eye for an opportunity, and so, it turned out, was the Leader. The minister picks up the phone.

'*Rare.*'

Soon his secretary tiptoes into the room with a stack of documents that await the minister's signature. It has already been pre-witnessed and stamped on all of them. As his mind keeps wandering, the minister validates orders, confirms appointments, signs decrees into law. He uses a fountain pen that is probably fake, but a good fake, not cheap, given to him by his wife on the day of his swearing-in. It pleases him that she would not dream of wasting money on the so-called genuine article when a good fake will do. His children have not inherited that habit of thrift, and pride themselves on being able to tell even a good fake a mile off. Where is the tipping point, into decadence? They are by no meaningful definition rich, and for generations they have scrimped and saved, nor have they given the children the impression that they might be. It is in the air, it is in the water. The whole young generation, all across the continent, have suddenly broken with the ancient habit of thrift.

'Never buy the genuine article if you can avoid it,' the minister says.

The secretary simpers. What else can the poor man do, faced with this ministerial whimsy? The minister pats his arm to continue.

'Now this—' says the secretary, imagining his boss momentarily lost.

'Yes-yes,' says the minister, who conducts his functional reading in a different compartment of the brain.

The Leader comes from a line of middling businesspeople. A little rice trading, a little silk, always some debt dragging at the cart, and though connected to the great ethnic network no great asset to it. There might have been shares held in some clandestine enterprise or another through the wives' or mothers' lending circle, but nothing to inspire much awe. When the Leader went into the force, that was by all accounts considered a step up in the hacking order. In this they are much the same.

Then how is the wife to be explained? The Leader is in a way a man without charm, in a nation of charming people. Ungainly also, with the long torso and the low-slung arse and the big cuboid head with the baby features and the sphincter-like little mouth. Surely that sleek, plump, catlike woman could have resisted an arranged marriage, had she wanted to. Yet it was her own father, a genial old brute in the force, who helped the future Leader rise swiftly through the ranks, and even sent him abroad to some fifth-tier doctorate mill. The future Leader had—let us be clear—no talent, no charm, no social skills. He had never had a friend he did not need to buy. He tended to grovel abjectly in one direction and sneer in the other, and take the devious path if it at all opened up. He was, in short, no good.

Then what? She must have seen it, the moment their eyes met across the university campus, that he would stop at nothing and had no shame. That he was a weapon that could be wielded, a loose cannon that needed pointing, an unstoppable force that, properly directed, would be the making of her and her entire clan. The terrible, unquenchable need. And the girl met his eye, across the campus, without wincing or flinching, as no other girl ever had. What that must have cost her, no one will ever know; perhaps it cost her nothing. And though she loved to laugh and had a plump ticklish body, she made her decision in an instant: to forgo the comfort and companionship so many seek in marriage, to say nothing of love, or sexual gratification, and plumb instead for advancement and prosperity, her own and her entire clan's. Her siblings can have been no use, a chin- or spineless lot; she must have known from an early age that these duties would devolve on her. And she met the ungainly youth's devious baby eyes without wincing or flinching, and of course he was hers from that moment on.

And throughout the long dry middling years in the force, the slow dribble of tea money—because no matter how bent an officer, there are limits to the wealth he can amass—she stood steadfast and never wavered. Yes, an extraordinary woman. And bore him the children too: perhaps they were a comfort to her; perhaps that is why she spoiled the chinless son with the chicken hair, like a lap dog. Opportunity did not come knocking until they were well into middle age. But when it came, it found her crouched and waiting, sleek, plump and ready to pounce and, once unleashed, as swift and limber and deadly as the first day.

'No,' says the minister.

The secretary rears back. 'These are merely—'

'A formality, yes. But it would seem—'

The secretary, poor fellow, is a-flutter. Really the minister wonders sometimes why he is forever surrounded by these old women, in male guise. Perhaps it is old women alone over whom he can be said to hold any sway.

'The august—' says the secretary, stirred in some region that lies too deep for tears.

The minister has no time for this. 'There is a wisdom,' he says briskly, 'in your superiors that is not yet in you. They do not require instruction in the matter of duty, even though—' he relents and pats his arm again '—they are grateful for the excellent work you do in such areas—'

The minister can feel a tremor of fear going through the secretary's whole body, and yet the fellow keeps coming. It will not do to underestimate these old women, once roused to indignation. The minister sighs.

'It will be processed by and by,' he says. 'You must be patient, or if you cannot be patient you must obey. I shall not, at this moment, on this day, so soon after this government—' he means himself '—has taken a drastic line on such offences, recommend—how many is it?'

'Three-thousand, two-hundred and seventy-one, but most—'

'Thank you. This government—' he means himself '—cannot be seen to recommend for the annual amnesty three-thousand, two-hundred and seventy-one offenders, among whom many, though by no means, as you say, all, are atoning for the very offenses on which this government has lately been taking a strong line. *Mere formality* though it may be.' He looks the secretary straight in the eyes. 'This document, having got lost somewhere among the lower ranks, what with the recent upheavals there as we have rooted out—'

The secretary seems to relax a little.

'By and by,' the minister reassures him, 'it will turn up. If there are urgent demands from above, it will no doubt be possible, after a thorough search, to recover it and process it through the proper channels, by which it will eventually reach me. I would not be surprised if in that event it could not somehow be expedited, or prioritised, or otherwise be got ready in time for the august—'

The secretary bows at the waist.

'Yes?' says the minister, still keeping a steady eye on him.

'Of course,' says the secretary.

Knock, knock, knock, said opportunity at long last to the future Leader, one late steamy evening at a restaurant along the river. One must imagine the twinkling lights, the ruins of dinner, the battery of empty bottles on the tin serving tables. A whiff of organic corruption in the air. The future Leader, a little drunk, exudes the strange mixture of brutality, gauche bonhomie and obsequiousness that identifies policemen the world over. All evening he has been eager to impress, in all three respects: he is a dangerous enemy, he is a man of the world, and he can help; when all is said and done there is nothing he cannot do.

What the foreigner is after is someone he can bribe and trust. He is a brash man, the foreigner, noisy, with a pale, doughy face and the sloppy deliquescent flesh you see in so many ageing Caucasian men. A single vast sweat stain darkens two-thirds of his shirt from chest to back. All evening he has alternately sung the praises of this country and its wonderful traditions, in ill-informed references, and vented his contempt for its people. The future Leader has agreed with him, emphatically. In doing so he has sometimes lost track of the argument and veered into irrelevance. We must imagine him already incontinent in his speech habits. The foreigner may be ill-informed, and moreover ill-suited to the climate, but he has always brought him back; there is between men of a certain kind a bond that bridges gulfs of culture, race and social ineptitude. They have in short sized one another up and found that they can work with one another, to their mutual and several advantage.

The foreigner has also, it became clear between slurps and gulps, amid the gun salvoes of hard laughter, between insinuations and gross profanity, *done his homework.*

'I have done my homework,' the foreigner has several times asserted, truthfully.

Not only does the foreigner have a comprehensive grasp of the business, complete with estimates ten years down the line, he is also fully on top of the legal situation, at least as far as the letter of the law is concerned. A business plan has been completed, the market research carried out. And though the scheme may be bold, there is nothing reckless about it. The plan is to bring *communication* to this country before, as it were, communication has come to this country, so that when communication comes to this country, it will find communication already there. Certain equipment will be imported, certain licenses and concessions gained, so that when the big slow operators at last move in, it is through the foreigner and, by extension, the future Leader, that they will have to go—if indeed they are able to move in at all.

Across the table, the wife has been all purring charm,

talking chummily now to the foreigner's dubious companion, whose very presence at the table is an insult to her, and now pretending to be tickled pink by the men's vulgar deprecations of her sex. Several times she has erupted in throaty laughter. Only once has she caught the future Leader's eye, encouragingly. But whatever else he may lack, the future Leader has a head for figures, whether innate or acquired under his wife's patient tutelage, and it is at any rate clear that there is no risk.

The money is to be put up by the foreigner, while the future Leader will act—due to certain restrictions on foreign business operations under the law of the land—as a nominee and front and general facilitator. For this he will be amply compensated, and in return for the compensation he will sign away, in a separate arrangement, the nominal rights, entitlements and so forth of his position, to their mutual and several benefit. *Homework* or no homework, if the business fails it will be on the foreigner's head alone, and if it succeeds—oh, they will all be very, very rich.

10.

To seize the day; to pick out opportunity's knock amid the racket that accompanies the corrupt officer's life from dawn till dusk: these are admirable skills. And there can be no doubt that they heard it loud and clear the first time, though it is equally true that it grew louder and more insistent as time went by. In conference that night and over the following days and weeks—the mind for some reason shrinks from imagining these discussions—it became clear to the future Leader and his wife that this was not only, given the circumstances, the best offer they had yet had, but that it was perhaps the best offer anyone had ever had. Money for nothing, that is already too good to be true, and this was better.

The licenses were soon gained and the paths smoothed, for rather less than the foreigner had been led to budget, and the difference split between the future Leader and those who helped him, so that as an unexpected corollary he found his standing much improved among the officers of his graduation class. For perhaps the first time in his life, the future Leader found himself popular; not, perhaps, liked, since no one could like the poor man, but admired and respected, for perhaps the first time in his life, for the quality that people cherish above all others in this country, his generosity, or in the homely phrase: his good heart. And if any of his fellow officers found themselves with a lingering revulsion, they soon suppressed it as a sign that they themselves lacked that cherished quality, and almost persuaded themselves that they did like the future Leader after all. Nor did it take anything away from the future Leader's generosity, in the eyes of his fellow officers, that he was being good-hearted with someone else's money.

That was another pleasing corollary, the lesson that all largesse is equally welcome, regardless of its source. He has since put it to good use. Oh, they were full days, the days when he made his fortune; they burst their seams with their fresh experience and swelling insight, to say nothing of new acquisitions. It is from this time also that the Leader's notorious sleeplessness dates, his habit of squeezing from his numbered days every last drop of profitable activity.

There were, to be sure, moments of discomfort. Half-educated, overeager and given to off-colour banter at inappropriate times, the future Leader did not present to his best advantage with the foreigner's friends and business associates, whom his new position occasionally obliged him to meet. He was sometimes ignored, and sometimes condescended to, by these enormously fleshy or sleekly burnished men—they were all men—with their machine-gun salvoes of laughter, and more than once he thought he caught the foreigner, out of the corner of his eye, sneering over his head at an acquaintance when he let the incontinent speech apparatus loose. Once, he could have sworn, he saw the foreigner wink. He was soon comforted when the monthly statements came in, for the carefully distributed accounts, under the various names; it was only perhaps that these moments strengthened in him the determination to become inviolable. Wealth, he saw—and had it confirmed by the wife—was in itself nothing, or the bare beginning of something. What you needed, and what he was determined to get, was inordinate wealth, spectacular wealth, wealth so wealthy that if you never worked another day it would simply go on breeding wealth of its own accord, and if, say, half of it was taken away, you would still be so wealthy that no one would dare sneer at you ever again.

It might be said that this was when the future Leader

——

84

became a menace. That hardly happened overnight. But gradually, over the months and years, he became as they say a force to reckon with. It got so you had to factor him in. There was a spring in his step. His success spoke for itself. Woe betide a criminal suspect when the future Leader peeked into the interview room, not because there would be beatings but because the bribe would double. He acquired a reputation as a negotiator. He was approached for investment. He was owed. He gave to the selected poor. At events, he spoke, in his thin, high, grating voice, making promises in language that tended perhaps to the saccharine but nonetheless, or because of it, found an echo in the breasts of his listeners and produced a smattering of applause. The words *heart* and *love* tripped easily off his tongue, contrasting pleasantly with the tough talk more traditional officers barked into the microphone on these occasions. His mouth sphinctered coyly when he spoke them, and his eyelids fluttered. On birthdays and the New Year, he had to put up an awning in front of the house, for the many who came to propitiate him. Old women hung garlands around his neck.

The minister, no stranger to garlands from old women, snuffles. Yes, that must be the story. He has proof of none of this, but he was in the force long enough to have seen all the roads to distinction. A feeling grows up around a man, an aura. The name is overheard, then repeated, then spoken with a widening of the eyes. Something gravitates. He acquires a retinue. Good fortune is believed to arise from proximity alone—

A menace, yes, because his generosity wrapped itself around you like a squid, all probing tentacles and suckers. It was not that the future Leader kept a book, but there would have been a sense abroad that you had better remember the kindness he did you, because if you forgot— There would be no retribution, none at all; only perhaps an irregularity would turn up, the deeds to a house miscategorised, a plot of reserved agricultural land used for other purposes, an ancient planning law contravened. It could all be fixed, if you then recalled the kindness he did you: the heart was still good, only the manner this time was rather more brusque, the eyes hooded, the voice more grating, and you never forgot again.

Well, so it goes. Give a little man a little power and you create a monster.

The business, meanwhile, prospered. Would-be competitors, soon alert to the rich rewards of bringing communication to the country, not only found communication already in place, but found it so firmly emplaced that there appeared to be no further room for communication. So that if they wished to get in on the business, it was through the foreigner, and through him the future Leader, that they would have to go. The foreigner, and the future Leader, had the business all sewn up. The wife, a fair-minded woman where business was concerned—though monumentally stupid, the minister reminds himself, with regard to the chinless son—gave the foreigner his due and sang his praises. There was a glint in her eye and a dimple in her cheek. She curled up on the new valanced sofa at the new mansion, in her parquet-friendly cloth slippers. Her manicured toes twinkled. She knew that nothing would goad the future Leader more than hearing her sing the praises of another man, especially another man who had been caught sneering, by her husband, at her husband.

In conference— No, the imagination shrinks.

The Leader, at any rate, had long absented himself for extended periods from the police department to which he was then still attached, and taken little interest in its day-to-day running. This was widely accepted, because he brought in money in other ways. He had become a vital link with the business community, and ensured a steady stream of fresh income from new ventures—the night clubs, the electronics malls, the financial institutions. But now something was brewing. Now he could often be seen at the department, or in cavernous seafood restaurants nearby, sitting up late into the night with his fellow officers. He had acquired a gaggle of lawyers, who shadowed him to these events: quiet, polite, highly educated men whose calm demeanour belied their nimbleness in negotiating the obstacle course, or maze, or some such metaphor, of the law of the land.

And here was a remarkable thing: the future Leader's inferiority complex—for that is surely what it is—could invariably be stilled by the simple expedient of getting his betters on his payroll. He was never intimidated by the lawyers, nor later by the financial wizards, the MBAs, the experts in satellite technology, so long as he paid them. He did not then jabber, or mince, or otherwise embarrass himself. And more, he quite calmly accepted their advice, perhaps from a sense that they occupied a department that he had had the wisdom to delegate, and that in giving good advice they in a way proved the wisdom of his decision. In this he was no doubt correct.

At these nocturnal meetings, at any rate, a course was plotted, a strategy agreed. Emerging replete from these gatherings no one spoke, but a tense, festive atmosphere hung about them. They smoothed their tight shirt fonts and breathed deeply of the air. Everyone could see that something momentous hung in the offing. And then one morning it broke.

Officers who had never been seen at the department before lunchtime gathered there at the crack of dawn, brisk, freshly showered, alert. A whole battalion was mustered in the morning mist. Uniform buttons gleamed, weapons sat squat in their holsters. Radios crackled. Positions were taken.

The foreigner had many admirable qualities, among them that he was a workhorse, and first in the office every day. No matter how swollen the eyes and how greasy the sheen on his forehead, he was at his post. This morning, too, found him in the office first up, planning, checking, overseeing, performing the vital acts of quality control. Then the drumming of boots down the hallway, the doors flung open, the glaring overhead lights flickering on. A rush of fierce energy suffusing the premises. Some thirty-five officers filed in and fanned out at once around the office. The foreigner sat stunned at his desk, all hard eyes on him, none of them meeting his. Then the senior officers marched in, in double column. Orders were barked, and obeyed in practised motion. Equipment was secured, files seized, before he had time to recover, jump up and demand in his loud, broken, uncouth voice to know what the hell was going on.

The future Leader, to his regret, stood out of sight in some anteroom and directed the operation. He had wanted to march in ahead of the force, on ringing boots, but the lawyers had advised against it, and he saw the wisdom. He did not, therefore, see all blood drain from the foreigner's face and leave him a sallow, trembling sack. He did not see the tainted sweat break out, nor witness him bent double over the desk by a pair of intent officers, nor hear the hard ratchet as the handcuffs bit into his wrists. It was only when they marched him out that the future Leader caught, barely out of the corner of his eye, the shocked, pleading expression in his business partner's eye, the flicker of hope, the flicker of doubt, the final understanding spreading across the loose features—

And so it was that the future Leader became the tycoon we know today.

The dawn raid, the minister thinks, was a masterful touch. Every officer loves the dawn raid, and the minister, for all his desk-bound history, is no exception. His nostrils flare. Only at the dawn raid is the officer truly alive. The dawn raid sustains him in the long tedious hours of producing documents in triplicate, of hanging around, of collecting cash from the business community ahead of the festive season. Memories of the dawn raid sustain him in retirement. Ah, the dawn raid! That, and the shootout, though you do not get those so much any more. In his own campaign, the minister has been careful to authorise any number of dawn raids, to bring the officers on side. Even his own night raid, that widely televised and profoundly satisfying event, which so profoundly affected such large, visible numbers, could not match the thrill of the dawn raid: the exercise of pure power, the dazzled victim, the swift finality of planned manoeuvres—

The foreigner, after a suitable period in gaol—suitable to arrange the requisite transfer of funds, but not so long as to create a panic among the foreign business community—was indicted under the ordinance pertaining to non-nationals running a company through a nominee or nominees, bailed and shipped at night across the river into a neighbouring country, which last cost him a considerable portion of his capital. The minister knows the cells; they are no better or worse than you would expect in this part of the world. You are kept barefoot, to discourage running. Sleeping space, on the polished cement floors, is at a premium, the lavatories tend to back up, but the ceiling fans work for hours at a time and the lust for violence goes straight out of people. They are quiet places, the cells. Food, if not plentiful, is adequate. Extra rations can be arranged, cigarettes delivered. The guards are brisk but dispassionate. No, gaol was not the worst of it. It was being hounded out of the country that by all accounts broke the man, with no prospect of ever being let in again, given the transparent justice of the indictment, and the breach of bail conditions. Or not even that, but that he became a laughing stock, to his associates at home, another patsy, the victim of an obvious Third World scam. When he did in truth have a genius for business—

No, the Leader leaves no perceived slight unavenged, nor a favour unpunished. Crush or be crushed, that is the primitive choice before the minister. Or there is a third choice, abject ingratiation, but the minister knows he does not have it in him to ingratiate himself to that extent. Unlike the Leader, it strikes him, who got on at first by abject ingratiation, and gets on by abject ingratiation still, in certain circles, to say nothing of his saccharine speeches to the People, than which no more abject ingratiation can be imagined. Oh, the jabbering of *love* and *heart*, in the thin, whiny, grating voice, twice Saturdays on the radio, for a full hour. Something fluting also, a kind of audible puckering of the mouth around those words. The minister, alone again in his office, pulls a face and spits into the wastepaper basket. Crush or be crushed: that is the choice before him. He leaves the back way.

11.

And now she is launched. And the Supreme councillor, massive, immobile, golden, at the still centre of their wheeling world, is launched with her. Wheeling, yes: she may be a streetwalker, but she does not like to walk, preferring by far the cheap indulgence of the motorbike taxi, riding side-saddle, ladies-fashion, legs on air. Can she really be a streetwalker still, at this age, which must be going on forty, with the boil, and the baseball hat on her bad hair? Still she comes out here, night after night, among the brilliant lights.

Oh, beautiful! The brilliant lights, the press of bodies, the cars nose-to-tail, the great space-age police box with the upside-down pyramid roof— Behind it, under day-bright fluorescent, hang, sit and stand hundreds of cheap suitcases, holdalls, rucksacks, handbags, wallets, in black and red and yellow polyester, all wrapped in glistening cellophane, a great proud testament to the regional light industry, its famous knockoffs, the nameless toiling numbers. All over the pavements, vendors have laid out their wares, printed t-shirts, plastic toys, sets of Tupperware, cooking tools made from coconut shells, and more wallets still, though all the wallets in the world cannot hold the money that changes hands here, because nothing can hold it, because all is flow—of money, of people, of bodily fluids, of drink—and the one imperative that nothing must stay still. Here all is turnover, circulation, motion. Drinks are poured into glasses, are poured down gullets, are emptied into urinals, are flushed into sewers, are washed to sea. The bags are forever packed. And the money too percolates, upwards, downwards, sideways, in endless spinning cycles, and the pistons pump, and the hearts beat, and the wheels turn—

Yes, that is the tone to take, thinks the supreme councillor, because we are here, the woman and I, to celebrate; though what it is we celebrate we do not rightly know. Head- and tail lamps blaze in the slick black tarmac. We take our regular seat, at the bent tin table by the all-night chemist's, by the grilled-chicken stall, by the car-park exit of the big three-star hotel, we join the two women from the old hut, and others too—hello, hello, with a kind word or a joke or a pat on the arm for everyone—young, beautiful, makeup at last coming into its own, in the brilliant glare from the fluorescent tube that has been fixed by God knows whom to the pylon. The nightly party.

And if every night could be a party, thinks the supreme councillor, then life need never end and could go on whirling, as the universe whirls, for all eternity. Perpetual motion, thinks the supreme councillor, that is the secret of the universe. Because what powers, for example, this fluorescent tube, strung with wire and twine to the leaning concrete pylon, but the whirling night itself, which is powered in turn by the thousands of lights illuminating it? What powers life but life? And is it not remarkable, also, that there are certain places where the moral universe is the universe as it exists? That on a corner like this, where a thousand crimes, as the books define them, are committed every minute—hello the two meat-faced officers, collecting their envelope from the bar manageress; hello the jittery fellow with the overhand handshake; hello the white gentleman upstairs, the top of his freshly showered old head just visible in a shard of light—all is as it is and is right and true?

On his many travels, the supreme councillor has found life right and true in the hazy fields at dusk, by cooking fires in the murmuring night, in the still hard streets when the shutters are down, or at dawn, when the great vans with the chicken crates stacked three metres high— Yes, has found life right and true everywhere, except perhaps around certain emblems of power, the emptiness, say, of the vast exercise yards, where he spent so many years of his undistinguished career, where a small crack in the paving can suddenly absorb all your attention, or the monuments on the great roundabouts, vast vortices of meaning—

Here we sit, at the nightly party. The women pick at their shared food: although they have already force-fed themselves, there must be food to feed the conversation, to give the hands and mouth something to do. The nails like gorgeous claws. The glistening mouths. They clink their glasses, mostly ice and water with a little rum to fire them up. Friends pass, fights erupt, drunks lurch, enormous transsexuals fret and preen. Already the story of her son's misfortune with the motorbike, retold, is taking on the qualities of folklore. The women scream with laughter, and she with them, at the lucky escape and the stupid skid, then grow all pious and sad at his prospects. It is not that they care; it is not that they do not. They will seize on anything for their enjoyment, and enjoy whatever they seize on.

They eye up with kinder eyes than ours the scrubbed, boiled, inflated white men who pass in their hundreds, but follow their passage with sharper tongues. And the hollow-chested shambling ghosts, with their dead-thatch hair and dusty clothes, their hiking boots. Always the hiking boots, what can that mean? They do not hike, these men, they would not last a minute in open terrain before they succumbed to a coughing fit or some terrible haemorrhage of the vitals; it is as if they had packed all sturdiness and resilience into their boots, to leave the rest brittle and sorry and frail. And yet we should not ignore the message of the boots, because these men are more resilient than they look, and they have been this poorly, this brittle, for many years without degenerating any further. For a moment, while the women talk and drink, the supreme councillor is tempted to follow one or the other of these men instead, to dip kingfisher-fashion into their frail souls, but he stays, they are distractions, and it is better to let distractions distract you than to home in on them.

Has he hit on something there, in the casual flow of his thoughts? Among the monks, distractions are greatly despised, and the whole world is in the last analysis distraction. Such foolishness. The error is not in becoming distracted, but in latching on to a distraction, barnacle-fashion, as though salvation were to be found in any fresh and undistracted concentration: hence the high priests of television, the proselytes of motor vehicles, the worshippers of money. Hence experts. To have a head for facts and figures, that is perhaps the worst fate that can befall a man. In another life the supreme councillor (thinks the supreme councillor) would have made a marvellous religious leader, preaching tirelessly among the poor against the facts and figures. Or else among the rich, it does not matter, they would all have benefited equally. Instead, he has become a kind of living deity, and a god does not speak or, if he does, speaks in riddles and mysteries.

But who comes here? A sallow fellow, undeniably tall, undeniably gangly, with an unmistakable hint of something gone to seed or pot. Early promise betrayed, a trajectory gone awry. Mouth: full. Smile: winning. Teeth: crooked. Shy eyes that never meet yours. But charming still; you can tell they are all fond of him, perhaps for the compliment he pays each one of acknowledging her singularity, and laughing at it. He takes the crane-like girl's wrist with exaggerated care, as though it were at risk of snapping under his fingers.

'What is the matter?' he asks. 'You do not eat?' As if the question had never been asked before.

'I eat,' she protests, as though for the first time. 'I eat all the time.'

'Eat more,' he says. 'Thin people: no good.' This from a man who has hardly more flesh on his bones than her. 'Nobody likes thin people. I want you fat, like me.'

The others laugh and shout compliments on his figure. The maternal woman pats him on the skinny stomach. 'Like pregnant,' she says. 'How many months?'

'Six.'

'Whose is it?'

'Yours and mine.'

'Oh? Why can I remember nothing?'

'You were drunk,' he says. And turning confidentially to the others: 'And so was I.'

They laugh again and invite him to sit and share their rum. He takes a plastic stool but announces, 'I cannot stay long.'

'You like us no more?'

'I love you,' he says. 'But there is somewhere I have to be.'

A woman, they decide. What else can it be? He makes a great show of coyness.

'Is she beautiful?'

He takes a slow sip of his rum-and-water. 'She is not ugly.'

They make a high-pitched sound not unlike *neee* that seems to express everything from envy at his good fortune to a suspicion that there is more to it than he cares to admit.

He laughs quietly. *Neee*, he says into his drink.

Hello, thinks the supreme councillor, here is a sorry fellow who nonetheless delights like us in the playful rituals. Vain, to be sure, and even at this sorry stage in his trajectory greatly in love with himself, or not so much perhaps in love as compelled, but for that reason compelled, too, by all that passes between him and others, the endlessly refracted sparkle of self and selves. And the supreme councillor utters the blessing, in his quasi-divine capacity: let no great harm come to him, and may whatever old grief cages and cossets him fade to a mere shadow by and by.

And not before time, because now the young—the youngish—man turns to the woman with an intent look on his face.

'Have you got any of the—' he says.

'*Rare.*'

He laughs. 'Is that yes or no?'

'What do you think?'

'*Rare.*'

'So how many?'

He holds up three fingers. 'Four.'

Unperturbed she makes a give-me gesture, and he takes a few banknotes from his wallet and pushes them across the table. She looks up left, then right, then slips them into her pocket.

'Excellent execution,' he says. 'Nobody would suspect a thing.'

'Why?' she demands. 'Who is looking?'

He sighs. 'Well, go on then.'

'Wait.'

They wait. The conversation goes hither and yon. The thin man's thin leg jiggles. Oh dear, thinks the supreme councillor, he really has very little self-control, but then he realises that the thin man is doing it on purpose, pointedly, to tell the woman to get on with it. She sighs and gets up.

'Also,' the man calls after her, 'you owe me money.'

She snarls. Heading across the car park she passes a gaggle of girls with bottles of alcoholic lemonade in their hands. Before them stand two of the boiled-looking men, barely more than boys, with military haircuts, in beach shorts and bathroom slippers, swaying to and fro and drawing circles on the tarmac with their delicate white toes. Who is wooing whom is impossible to say. She walks into the lobby; the fluorescent inside is day-bright too, refracted in veneered and laminated furniture. Here and there sit men and women, alone or in groups, as in a sort of anteroom of life, waiting their turn. Clocks purport to tell the time in the world's major cities, though it seems odd that they should differ by twenty-two minutes on top of the hours, in aggregate. All through the long lobby she walks, then sharp left by an empty vase into a panelled suite of lavatories. She locks herself into a cubicle and extracts the plastic bag from her bra, counts four into her hand and wraps them in toilet paper, then secrets the bundle in an empty sweet wrapper from her bag. Then she dials a number, lets it ring three times, hangs up. And out again on the long march back to the table.

The man sits hunched now, smoking furiously. Well, it takes as long as it takes, he should be used to it by now. She sits down.

'And?'

They perform the same manoeuvre as before, but in reverse: looking up and around, left and right—only this time she catches the eye of an officer who has positioned himself at the entrance to the car park, behind the young-ish man's back. The officer nods and shifts a leg into the watch position.

The man smiles dazzlingly, takes a long last gulp of his drink, slaps both hands flat on the table and stands up.

'Time,' he says, 'waits for no man.'

He nods in the round; they acknowledge him or not. Then he strides briskly off toward the corner, where the motorcycle taxis sit and wait. The officer, now joined by a second, hurries after him, something childlike in their intentness, a kind of tunnel vision. The busty friend raises an eyebrow, but the

97

woman is occupied with the ice cubes and the visor of her baseball hat hides her eyes.

The night wears on. Many more men pass; some also sit down. The lights sparkle, the sound systems from the two open bars opposite clash at the precise point where the women sit, perpetually refusing to resolve themselves into one or the other song. It would be maddening were it not, in the last analysis, the same noise, doubled, a generic syncopated clamour of fun and life, a great aural bulwark against the dark. They shout, chatter, moan, they keep up a steady flow of complaints and jokes, and they rarely know which is which. Then out of nowhere a vigorous fellow, with a bald head like a snooker ball, hugs as many of them as he can in vigorous stubbled arms. A yelp and cheer goes up. And yes, he has come, as they hoped and prayed, to take them all away to a party, in his room, or rooms, at a nearby hotel. That is them taken care of, for the night. And as they gather their things and signal the old woman at the drinks cart for their bill, her phone goes.

'*Rare.*'

'Idiot,' says the voice.

'What?'

'Idiot. After all these years you send the swine after *me*?'

'What are you talking about?'

'How stupid do you think I am?'

'Stupid.'

'Yes, well, but not stupid enough for them.'

'What happened?'

'They went one way, I went another, what do you think?'

'I cannot hear what you say. Now I go.'

'Fine. But you still owe me money.'

She clicks the phone off and grins. On his solitary wedding bed, the supreme councillor chuckles and goes to sleep.

12

Sleep within sleep within sleep. He has no idea where he is now. How pleasant that is. Knowing and not knowing, pleasant. The familiar and the unfamiliar. Though all experiences, even the most unfamiliar, are familiar, or else we would not be able to experience them. His mind keeps up its pleasant murmur, even here. He has an impression of extraordinary quiet, and his mind quietly murmuring, like grass. There are no people here. Is that it? Nothing but the grass and the trees, and the creatures of the grass and the trees, for miles and miles around. No living people. Is that it? Some backwoods sage said all animals are asleep, that is the difference between them and people. No one awake, except the supreme councillor, who is asleep. He is the grass and the trees of the sleep-world, and the creatures of the grass and the trees, the soft murmuring cover of the sleep-world, where all that has been lies becalmed, under gentle mounds of earth. Is that it? No people, no living people, only dead people, becalmed people, people at last at rest.

A world without people would seem, to people, extraordinarily quiet. Extraordinarily calm. And yet the creatures go about their murmuring business, and the grass and the trees grow and are stirred by the wind and fed by the nutrients from the soil. The creatures murder the creatures they need to feed them, which in turn murder other creatures to feed them, and great predators circle overhead, with their baby cries. If you put your ear to the ground you would hear the great churning wrenching sound of the plants dragging themselves up from the soil, incessantly. You would hear them withering on the wind, incessantly. And the death throes of the murdering animals, and the crunching, squelching mandibles. And yet the impression is of a great quiet, an extraordinary calm. Because the people are gone at last. Is that it? Has he come to witness the end-times, with their perpetual pristine beginnings? There should be ghosts. There are no ghosts.

It would not surprise the supreme councillor, that he of all people should be chosen to witness the end-times, as one who would appreciate them. Yes, to a god the end-times would have to reveal themselves, that would only be fit and proper; a god might well take exception if the end-times refused to reveal themselves to him. A god might well be expected to inhabit the end-times, their grass and the creatures of their grass, spreading himself like a soft blanket over times past, and struggles done, and the long sleep of everything. Perhaps there are other gods here, all spreading themselves quietly over everything forever.

How tedious, the end-times! Their ineffable quiet, their implacable calm. The arc of existence always ends in tedium, that is one of the great laws of the universe. He has forgotten the others. Perpetual motion? Yes, and one or two more. At one time the old house was a place of life and conviviality, of coming and going. He had many friends; they were artists and statesmen, they were women of society. Some were fierce critics of the regime of which he was perhaps the staunchest pillar. All spoke their mind. Foreigners too, the better kind: diplomats, writers, movie people, figures of some small influence. All the foreign correspondents would come to see him. They thought of him as an oracle, they believed him *outspoken,* and he found them attentive enough. Now of course they no longer come; they want to see the bankers. It is their loss, for there is no more tedious liar than a banker. At least the supreme councillor lied with charm and wit, and sometimes gave them a nugget of truth, if he liked them. They usually missed it and would have written lies anyway.

He was fond of one in particular, an absurd fellow who dressed all in white and wore a great walrus moustache that must have been hell in the heat. He was forever hinting at his philandering ways, as though in this country that were anything to write home about. Yet he had been there at the great cataclysmic events of the region; he had what they call a *nose,* and he had such lively eyes and such beautiful gestures, and his contempt for facts and figures almost matched the supreme councillor's own. If you told him a phrase in the language, he repeated it with great enthusiasm and wrote it down wrong. Impatient also, easily bored, and as full of opinions as a sack of fighting cocks. And yet for all that some kind of sage or seer, who often got by misdirection to the heart of the matter. Yes, they spent some pleasant evenings here in the old house, laughing and out-windbagging each other.

The old house for so long was a place of laughter and conviviality. He had a pack of cheerful dogs that he loved. At parties the guests wandered among the flame trees, lanterns swayed in the evening air overhead, and their drinks were refreshed from long trestle tables set up along the pond. The artists and statesmen, the women of society. The wry critics of the regime. They dressed in light, simple clothes. They came here to leave the rigours of the world behind. Cook produced one delicious dish after another all night long, on her twin gas rings, listening to songs of heartbreak on her transistor radio. The outbuildings swarmed with staff.

For years a leathery old man squatted on a dry patch just inside the gate, with his tin cart from which he sold skewers of grilled chicken livers and pork neck. He had rigged himself up an awning, and there he slept come rain or shine. Nobody knew his name. Nobody knew when he had arrived or who had given him permission to stay, but he bothered no one and did no harm. It was said that his wife had thrown him out and he had nowhere to go. But what of his earnings? Each afternoon he set out for the market, with his cart, and returned at nightfall. He washed from a garden hose, ate his dinner from a bowl, and stretched himself out on his camp bed, under a sheet that covered him from head to toe like a shroud. Only twice, at times of great floods, did they offer him a bed in the servants' quarters. He lay down without a word of thanks.

One morning they found that he had died in his sleep. All he had in his possession was a few coins and a scrap of paper with a telephone number, which turned out to be the waterworks. The supreme councillor paid for the funeral rites. The cart, for all he knows, still rusts on the dry patch by the gate, and the maids put out a plate of offerings to his ghost, a glass of white spirit, a cheroot, a piece of cake, though nobody had ever seen him drink or smoke.

Yes, the convivial days are gone. Instead the reverent hush, and the animal sounds: the whoop-whoop of the coucals as they limp though the canopies, the plaintive cuckoo's dying fall, the cicadas, the bullfrogs. The foreign correspondents no longer come; or perhaps they still come but the attendants turn them away. No matter. All the livelong day the question before him has been in which of a thousand possible ways to do nothing. It is only fit and proper that he should by and by spread himself over the end-times like grass, eternally murmuring with no one to listen to him, doing nothing forever.

The ghosts perhaps are still here but maintain a respectful silence. No doubt the attendants shush them, if they make a noise. The supreme councillor knows that he has to a great extent become dependent on the attendants. They are his eyes and ears, also his hands and mouth. They are his enormous invisible feet. They interpret his utterances for the world, and the world's utterances for him, by and large. He trusts them entirely. He does not entirely trust them. They are as powdered and perfumed a bunch of toadies as ever walked the face of the earth; they speak softly and walk softly and tremble like curtains stirred by the wind at the approach of any disturbance. They let no disturbance reach him. They let no harm come to him. Hence perhaps his nocturnal excursions, to keep his wits about him and see for himself what is afoot in the land, unmediated by the attendants' soft perfumed instincts, their gentle dissembling.

Since when has he become so dependent on the attendants? Perhaps it has always been thus. Yet at one time he bestrode the world with vigour, even though it was his mission above all to do nothing, in a thousand possible ways. He has vivid memories of the great decorated uniform, the enormous boots. He could see his toad-face in the boots when they were freshly shined, and in each of the dubious medals, each of which he richly deserved. Each medal was a little shiny milestone in his lifelong campaign to do nothing. The Order of the Garter. The Order of the Sleeve. The Order of the Pillow. The Order of the Lunch. Was there ever a more decorated chest in the whole of this nation than when the supreme councillor stepped out on the stand to address the troops? He knows the history of each of his medals and when it was first awarded, roughly. It is not that he has a great curiosity about them, but that that is the sort of information a man like him can be expected to pick up. Nothing is lost in the supreme councillor's memory. The correct way to tie the sash. The regulation width of the buckle. If he is not mistaken he designed the new guards' uniform himself, one idle afternoon while the dogs snoozed at his feet, how long ago now?

Where are the dogs now? They never bark.

Yes, he strode vigorously, and he strode alone. He prided himself, in his proud days, on a certain independence. His friends—the society women, the statesmen, the critics of the regime—came by and large from great families of the land, and their names rang with fulsome tradition. Whereas the supreme councillor comes in a way from no family at all. He has a notion that he was born out of wedlock, though that has not been confirmed. The monks found him when he was a few weeks old, on the relevant steps, and took him in. Well, they could hardly leave him out there. He was made a ward of the state, and brought up by the monks, whom he has ill repaid for their kindness, for from the earliest days religion bored him. How ironic, then, that he should now be turning into a god. As a young lad he teased and heckled them, and well into old age he could not fully suppress his impatience in their company. He has shirked his duties in that line, religiously. On certain occasions he has deliberately diverted funds; on others he has encroached on religious land.

To the state, on the other hand, whose ward he became, he has always been grateful, though he became its ward in name only and the state did nothing to deserve his gratitude. Perhaps that is what he has been grateful for. The non-interference of the state: that became, at a certain point, the great principle of his career. It remains his principle to this day. Yes, he has served the state for most of his life, in one capacity or another, selflessly, or selfishly only insofar as it pleased him above all to serve the state. It would be no exaggeration to say that he became, at a certain point, the state, or that his life became so bound up with the state's as to make the two of them indistinguishable. And yet the state's yoke has been easy, all his life, and such small merit as he has accumulated consisted of keeping the state's yoke easy for everyone else. Though there were a handful of executions, that is only to be expected.

As with music, so with the state. The great old masters sit all but motionless at the instrument; only beginners and amateurs throw themselves frenziedly about and disturb the very trees with their antics. The great politicians too—and the supreme councillor is perhaps the greatest politician this nation has ever seen—reach by and by a state of perfect equilibrium, in which they no longer seem to be influencing the course of affairs at all, but merely permit affairs as it were to course through them, undisturbed. And yet without them there would be chaos. It is as if their very stillness, their very inactivity, had a calming, channelling, subliming effect on the chaotic cross-currents of affairs, which simply by passing through that centre of stillness, that core of inactivity, resolved themselves into harmony.

Oh, but it takes an instrument of extraordinary sensitivity to achieve that state. Or a player of extraordinary sensitivity, it does not matter; they are, in a great musician or a great politician, the same. A great politician must make all the joys and pains and concerns of all the people in the nation his own. He suffers and rejoices with each man, woman and child in the nation, and is yet indifferent to all of them. He swells with the nation's triumphs and wanes with its defeats, yet allows neither triumph nor disaster to unhinge him. Above all, he embraces; it is in his arms that the nation is at peace, to his breast that it wearily returns, in his eternal shade that it rests.

Hence the end-times: no wonder. And yet, what

unutterable tedium, here among the murmuring grass, and the creatures of the grass, with their monotonous cycles. What nameless grief. You would be bored to tears forever, at the end-times; that it would serve you right is neither here nor there. Please, gentlemen—the supreme councillor addresses his own senses—I hear you loud and clear. You must not doubt for a moment that your message, as we politicians like to say, has got through. A need is being impressed on me, a call to action—good. Let us say no more about it. The message is understood, the call has found its echo in the enormous, golden, quasi-divine breast, which here swells calmly on the in-breath and sinks on the out-breath on the vast wedding bed, while the half-open toad lips tremble faintly, or seem to tremble in the flickering light, it is all the same, and the toes perhaps wiggle into a semblance of life. But first, gentlemen, if you do not mind, we must sleep.

13.

At dusk, if thanks be given, the day rewards us / For the rigours of our toil, writes the national poet, or words to that effect. This was towards the end of his life. The future minister could never, in his schooldays, reconcile himself to that claim, because what possible difference could it make to a natural phenomenon whether thanks were given or not? He understood what is called the tenor of the metaphor, but he did not understand the vehicle, and decided there and then that the arts were perhaps a fine ornament for the idle but no use to people like him, on whom it had been impressed from an early age that life was to be hard graft and ceaseless striving, eyes on the goal. Also he was unmusical. Crossing a public square he sometimes stopped dead because he mistook some marching song being played over the tannoy for the national anthem, and stood for seconds baffled that the stream of humanity around him refused to come to a halt. It was a vertiginous feeling, as though he had been transported to a foreign country, or the revolution had come overnight and he was the only one not to be told. He learned to look at his watch before stopping, since the anthem is played only at eight in the morning and six at night, the hour of dusk, when if thanks be given the day rewards us for the rigours of our toil.

The lines pop into his head as he climbs out of the ministerial car and, stretching, looks up at the sky. As omens go it is glorious, vast smears of cement grey across the most delicate blue, and even rows of fluffy white clouds travelling demurely east like a flotilla of cotton pads, while the sun, a huge copper coin, daubs their edges according to the distance in shades of gold and pink and purple. Well, it cannot hurt to give thanks, so the minister tips the sky a brisk nod before gathering the bag of grilled bananas to his chest and marching towards his front door.

It nearly flies open to meet him, as though unable to contain the multitudes that mill within. He recognizes some cousins from the wife's side, ungainly drab young things who greet him ducking their heads and smiling tentatively. He sketches a greeting in return and shoulders through. They are of no significance. In the middle of the sitting room, as though caught in a sunbeam, twirls his daughter. Stiff shopping bags sit and stand around her. She has been trying on the outfits, though not the wedding dress itself, which will be hired, and is parading them in front of family and friends. She twirls on her bare feet, instep turned slightly outward, showcasing what looks to the minister like a kind of sack.

He cannot be the first father, he often thinks, to suffer this soft, wincing shock every time he sees his daughter, at the beauty he and the wife have produced. There she gleams, in her slightly gangly, slightly watery way, the focus of all attention. She takes after no one, and this watery quality is really delicacy, and shyness, something loose and undefended, a reluctance to impress herself fully on your senses. Though her lips are thin: that is the heritage from both parents and cannot be overcome. At the same time she has a natural authority, there in the centre of the valanced sitting room, with its shades of powder-blue and taupe. None of the relatives comes even close, and they watch her with a kind of worshipful pride. The minister vaguely recognizes one of her friends among the shopping bags, a standard-issue pretty woman, slightly hard-faced, full of beans, who would come across well on television; but here his daughter almost turns her to furniture.

His daughter spots him now, and beams. Such extraordinary teeth young people have now. The wife will have a better idea of the cost; he must remember to ask. His daughter raises her slim white hands to form a greeting of appropriate humility. His lips stretch in a reluctant smile, and he advances, neck bent, into the circle that has formed around her. A polite 'Ah!' goes up among the friends and relatives, which he quells with half a dozen vague nods. Yes, in their different ways they form an appropriate focus for the worshipful pride, the minister and his beautiful daughter.

'You are getting ready for the festivities?' says the minister.

She simpers at the shopping bags. 'A little bit,' she says.

The minister is conscious of how much wheedling and cajoling is taken for granted in a daughter's relationship with her father. It can be seen daily on television, in the interminable, interchangeable soaps. His own sister did not wheedle; it is a recent phenomenon, or a symptom of racial integration, or social ascent, who knows. At least his daughter does it with a certain understatement. Of course it is efficacious either way, because if a father is not charmed outright he will yield from discomfort at these histrionics. The temptation to inquire about the cost is strong, but he bites it back. They can afford it. He becomes aware that a smile has frozen his features, halfway between pleasure and embarrassment, and wills his mouth into reptilian neutrality.

'Have you—' says his daughter, patting him impatiently on the chest with her tapering fingertips.

He nods. 'Feelers have been put out. Though it is too early to tell—'

She bounces on the balls of her feet. 'Oh,' she says pleadingly, 'but he will, surely.'

He is not at all certain. 'We shall see. There is the question of the amount which would satisfy—'

She clamps her hand over her ears. 'No, you must not say

things like that.'

He smiles thinly. 'Even if they are true?'

'Even then. It is not—'

'Appropriate?'

'Exactly.' She laughs. 'It is not appropriate.'

'Let us only say then that the supreme councillor is considering our request.'

She looks at him sideways. 'How much—'

He names the sum.

Her mouth forms an 'o'. 'But then he must surely—'

He cuts her off. 'As I say, we shall see. Now you will want to try on more of your purchases, and I must find your mother. Is—' He can never remember the fiancé's name.

'Oh, yes,' she says, pointing vaguely to the back of the house. 'I am sure he will be—'

'I am sure,' he says, and steps out of the charmed circle.

He finds his wife in the kitchen, where these days she always seems to be found. It is as if in advance of their daughter's wedding she was compelled to impersonate a housewife, implausible though she may look in the role; her pompadour, still at this hour, gives the impression of having been sculpted from shellac and glued to her head, and her jewellery suggests a stage. Maids withdraw on tiptoe to their quarters.

'Ah,' she says.

'Ah.'

'You remembered the bananas.'

He proffers the bag, which she drops on the table.

'The—'

'Yes, his *people*'—he spits—'are contemplating the sum,

apparently. These things take an inordinately long time, with these people.'

'Yes, well, we know that. So long as things are moving.'

'Oh, they are moving. Snail-wise.'

She nods. 'It will be worth it.'

'So you say.'

'Quite apart from the wedding, think what it can do for your prestige in the government.'

'Now supposedly at its height, yes. It may gratify you to hear that I was approached today, by some people—'

'Which people?'

He names a few names. She waggles her head, minimally, reserving judgment.

'Quite.'

'What did they want?'

'They indicated that were I to challenge for the leadership they might smile on it.'

She waggles her head again, though her eyes brighten a little and her posture becomes fractionally more alert.

'They have the money?'

'Quite. I am told they are the vanguard.'

'And if they are?'

'Then we shall see.'

She stares at him. 'We have had no further thoughts?'

'The day—' He lifts his chin.

'Ah?'

'The day will come when this—cooperation, for mutual benefit, with the Leader will have run its course.'

'Sooner rather than later maybe.'

'Quite.'

But her patience is at an end. She walks over to the kitchen cupboard and extracts a couple of bowls. She shakes the grilled bananas into one bowl and undoes the rubber band on the taut plastic bag with the treacle, which she expresses into the other. She dips a banana into the treacle and eats, then proffers the bowl.

The minister shakes his head no. A maid appears.

'Take these to—' the wife says, pointing her chin in the direction of the assembled clan.

'You are having no more?' says the minister.

'Diet,' she says.

'Ah.'

'But the money is somewhere behind this—vanguard?'

He shrugs. 'Is it?'

'It is a simple calculation,' she says.

He snuffles. 'No calculations in this country—'

'It is.' She flaps at an imaginary mosquito. 'Everyone knows that the Leader has bought this country. If they want to challenge, the only reason is that they see their pockets draining into his. I know you are an excellent minister, but that is the reason.'

'That, or they believe in magic.'

'Well—'

'Well?'

'They believe in magic, and they believe in money.'

'You mean the money takes precedence?'

'I do not know precedence, uncle. I am not an intellectual like you. But I know these people.'

'And?'

'If I look for magic, I find it.'

Her superstitious habits have been the subject of some banter over the years, and she plays the lottery religiously. On the other hand she always tends to be small sums to the good.

'You mean you look for it where it is likely to be found?'

'Not in the slums, yes.'

'Ah.'

'Though I knew a toothless old woman by the canal, who lived with her granddaughter and read excellent cards for

---

112

practically nothing. The girl's parents had died of the plague—
'
'Yes, well.' She means Aids. With that they seem, at any rate, to have arrived at an agreement, the wife and he, that all they can do is wait to discover who and what is behind the vanguard before they go any further. 'I remember that woman.'

'You arrested her.'

'Not personally; she came under the crackdown.'

Her face softens. 'Ah the crackdown—'

'You paid her fine.'

'She read me the cards for nothing for years after that.'

'And never a death or illness on the horizon.'

Snuffling freely, the pair of them look for a moment more like twins than husband and wife. Then she calls them to order.

'You have seen the—?'

'No. What *is* his name?'

She snorts again and tells him.

'Of course.'

'Ah.' She turns away, and he is left to find his future son-in-law.

More and more the young of his own world strike the minister as inordinately bland. But for the context he cannot be sure that he would have recognized the future son-in-law, an entirely generic creature, not un-gauche, not un-square, not unlike a dog in the way his eyes rest softly on your face. Does he have political affiliations? Has passion rippled his watery soul? Already he is wearing bathroom slippers over his socks,

113

like an old man. He has rather large flat feet. He met the daughter at university, where they studied in the faculty of accountancy. Already, during the obligatory stint abroad, they shared accommodation. No great upheavals seem to have marked their relationship; it is rather as if they slipped into it as you slip into a comfortable pair of trousers. They have a friendly, smiling way of dealing with one another.

All this is for the best. Further, that the son-in-law will in due course take over the family business, where he already plays a role of some consequence and has achieved a degree of expansion, into new markets. In a nation of people with thick enduring black hair, he is already going a little bald in front. A phlegmatic sort of sheep, he nonetheless has the acumen. Yes, the minister could hardly have hoped for a better son-in-law.

Respectful, too, as he now raises his hands in greeting, yet not obsequious, as people often are, given the minister's position. The impression of gaucheness, then, is misleading, a matter of large bones and perhaps lack of training in any physical discipline, rather than a symptom of discomfort in his own skin. In fact, the son-in-law occupies his place comfortably, because he does not see why he should not. No doubt he is subject to some good-natured ribbing from his contemporaries, which he takes equably. The paunch that is beginning to form above his nondescript, not overly expensive belt, is one such comfortable, humorous manifestation; in the family circle, the daughter can sometimes be seen patting it, in mock-admonition, to which he responds with a friendly yelp of protest. The impression, overall, is of a man who will stint nothing yet always live within his means. Their house will have marble floors but no wine cellar. That sort of thing—

The minister feels suddenly swamped by a wave of existential boredom. These matters have all been settled long ago.

'Ah,' he says, perhaps too abruptly, because the son-in-law

gives him a look of mild alarm. He makes to leave when the young man pipes up.

'Only—'

'Yes?'

'I was speaking today to my juniors—' he uses a general term. '—and they all said how happy they are with the work of this government, and Father's' —he means the minister's— 'and the Leader's in particular, so of course we are all very proud—' He smiles in his slightly doglike way. Perhaps he expects to be petted on the nose.

'Yes-yes,' says the minister, and makes to leave.

But the son-in-law is not done. 'Perhaps,' he says, slowly but inexorably, 'if the supreme councillor cannot after all be persuaded to preside at the wedding, the family wondered if it was at all possible that the Leader—'

'Listen,' barks the minister. How does the family suddenly come in? 'We shall see. These are busy men.'

Rudeness being the prerogative of men of the minister's standing, the son-in-law now simply relaxes, stands back and raises his hands. The minister, barely lifting a hand to chest-height, barges past him to the safety of his study.

These remarks, he thinks when he has caught his breath, are of course open to every interpretation. The son-in-law may have meant his staff, or he may have meant his juniors in the strict hacking order of his university days, so lightly adhered to all the livelong day, who may now be occupying positions of some consequence, in their respective enterprises. The general term admits of that meaning. He may have meant his younger siblings or other relatives. Equally he may set no great store by the Leader's work but perhaps caught the minister's weariness and wished to cheer him up. Perhaps it was another instance of the cajoling that informs the dealings of the younger generation with the older at every turn. Or it may after all have been a heartfelt expression of loyalty, to him, or the Leader, or both.

We must keep our ear to the ground at all times and be wary of believing anything it hears. The voice of the people is like any oracle, ambiguous, slippery, sly, but full of fervour too, a matter of some fifty million profound convictions forever un- or mis-expressed. Really it cannot be known before it has been called out. But once called out—oh then, for a man who knows how, the whole incessant jabbering cacophony can yet be made to ring like one clear bell.

14.

Drinking, smoking and cards, drinking, cards and smoking, these were the pastimes of the monks. Why would they not be? They were the pastimes of the farming class from which they came, and for that matter of the entire country. The supreme councillor's own tastes are eclectic and all-embracing, yet he is free of all vices except perhaps the vice of self-regard, than which there is in this country no more loathsome vice. Still, he is old enough to assess himself dispassionately, and has come to the conclusion that he fully deserves the regard in which he holds himself, because it is as nothing compared to the regard in which others hold him.

In the matter of cards, drinking and smoking, at any rate, the supreme councillor has never run with the herd. As a young man he tended to a certain moral intractability, born no doubt of insecurity, and of the need to set himself apart from his forest upbringing among the monks. One deep fragrant night, he and the other lads sneaked to the back of the sleeping quarters, where a crumbling old structure that smelt bitter with rot served as the den. Careful to avoid small twigs, they crept on bare feet through the tall grass, which no doubt teemed with snakes, to say nothing of the spirits that lived in this part of the forest, and through gaps in the loosely hung fabric they spied on the monks, in their fug. The boys' hearts were alive with the daring, and thudded to the great canopy of trees and stars above, and warmed to the glow of the oil lamp inside, where the monks sat cross-legged with their rum, and their woodbines, and their cards.

Thud, went the rotten floorboards; *slap*, went the cards; *clink*, went the glasses; *tushh*, went the matches.

They felt him, the spare one, an instant before he spoke, a

heavy dark looming presence, and their hearts, which had been as big as the sky, shrank in the instant to cold hard pebbles, and their throats dried and their hands shook.

'What do you think you are doing here?' the spare one said, in a rough, late-night, matter-of-fact voice.

Well, it taught them to count heads, at least. The slippers in those days were made from hard old tyres, and hurt worse even than the bamboo sticks the monks used in class, between imparting their sorry rote of old wives' tales.

Yet it was not for their brutality that he despised them, nor for their yokel ignorance, but for their complacency. The blank set faces. And now, he thinks, he has become more monumentally complacent than the worst of the idiots who brought him up. Did they know how much he despised them? He believes they did, and that it perhaps even smarted a little, through the fat hide of their complacency, but at the same time they were as superstitious as the next man, and felt him to be some sort of cursed or blessed being, a saint perhaps, or a devil, and spared him the worst of the rod and left him by and large to his studies.

At the same time they were in their way kind, and one or two of them had a—how would you put this?—a sort of narrow old forest-bound insight into the workings of the world, and the cycles of life. They tended their bean rows, lovingly. More is rarely needed. They fed the dogs too, that has to be counted in their favour, and they were by and large not after greatly enriching themselves. A hand-cranked radio maybe for the family, or a pig—were those the great desiderata of that era? Had the motor car come in by then? That sort of thing—

They lined up meekly enough for their dull duties, the sitting and recitations, and even the beatings were administered dutifully, for it was believed, in the forest, that who spared the rod spoiled the child, which would then grow up a prey to all the vices the monks themselves indulged, in their crumbling den. And though they had been beaten in their turn, it never occurred to them to put two and two together, or if it did they did not wish to upset the natural order of things

They were small people. That too has to count in their favour. Many of them had been born in the forest and never been further than the provincial town, with its main street and two cross-streets and its brand-new clock tower in front of the market. There was at one stage a veritable craze in the country for clock towers, perhaps so that the time they told on their four all-seeing faces would inculcate among the locals a habit of punctuality and industry in keeping with the modern age. But the results were dubious, and it was soon never the same time whether you came to market from east or west or north or south, and by and by they were no longer wound, and stood idle and peeling, shod in a single red mud-shoe that came up to your waist in the monsoon. There they still stand today, the supreme councillor fully believes, used now as makeshift electricity pylons, while the real centre of town has moved a kilometre one way or the other, to the supermarket, the motorcycle shops and banks, the sparkling thumping amusement compound. Though the clock towers warble the national anthem still, at eight in the morning and six at night, in their tinny, yammering voice.

They were all small people there, not just the monks, and told the time by the sun and the seasons, the great fat pregnant clouds that towered into the sky above the hills, the clank of the evening bell. They called out like plaintive birds at quitting time and went home to their huts, where they shifted and murmured into the night, and sank at last into sleep, in the one dark room they mostly all occupied, lulled perhaps by the waffle of their transistor radio. Now of course it is the television, but he fully believes the ancient rhythms are the same there still.

119

So the doctor, by comparison, was a big man there, one of two or three. Another was the local gangster, who had a logging firm besides one or two other interests, and was greatly revered at the house of worship, as the doctor was not. Yet it was the doctor who early took an interest in the future supreme councillor, and introduced him to his books, in return for a timid fumble now and again that he carried out with trembling hands.

These stories, the supreme councillor thinks complacently, are wholly generic, and that also must be count in their favour.

It was from the doctor, not the monks, that he got his education. Not much of a doctor, poor fellow, who invariably sent the patients away with a bag of penicillin and a bag of aspirin, whatever complaint they had come with. They mostly doctor like that still in the provinces. And while he may have done more harm than good, or equal harm and good, or some other mixture, medicine was not where his interests lay. No, the doctor's passion was for history and the arts, but in his day these were considered pursuits for the upper classes alone, and he came from a humble provincial family, who wanted his talent for book learning put to some use. What a sad man he was, despite the respect he enjoyed among the villagers! With his poor fumblings, which were really a watery overflow of the pedagogic Eros, and a mere trickle at that, a thin surfeit of what elation he was still able to feel at sharing his passions. And they came to an end soon enough.

All the doctor's earnings went on books, which he had sent from the capital and overseas, whence they would arrive after weeks and months and sometimes not at all. This was at the time more common in the Third World than it is today, this thirst for knowledge, even though the taste for educational qualifications has since exploded into gluttony. The doctor hinted that he had been abroad, though perhaps that was wishful thinking. More likely he travelled in his mind alone, and found only in his books adventure as well as consolation. From his tales, which the doctor really told himself, the future supreme councillor got his first sense of how nations might usefully be ruled, and how they might usefully not. Then he took to reading himself, in first two then three languages, and they would sit companionably on the doctor's tiled porch, by the light of the single bulb, under a fan that barely stirred the soupy air, reading.

Peep-peep-peep-pipipipipipi, said the plaintive cuckoo; s*ra-sra-sra-sra*, said the cicadas.

He got through the books at an enormous rate; such hunger as he had for life, and it was an enormous hunger, he thinks with wonder now, went at the time into his reading. Perhaps that is why he is so enormous still, here on the wedding bed, with the learning still rumbling around in his belly, in addition, admittedly, to heroic amounts of food, not to mention the triumphs and disasters of an entire country, over the centuries. Of course he remembers not a word of it, but he has a feeling that the wisdom and folly are still alive in him, under the thin shift that covers his recumbent form, and wiggle and ferment there still, a microcosm of the country, which none can be said to have ingested more fully than the supreme councillor.

The picture he formed of the world from his voracious reading was wholly erroneous. The world seemed a place at once of immense antiquity and strident modernity, where nothing had to be paid for and a great clear even light shone on all human deeds, both as to their consequences and their intrinsic moral value. It would in a way be true to say that his reading taught him nothing, even as it taught him everything. As a result of it, too, he soon left the other boys so far behind that they might as well have been inhabiting different worlds.

Yet he was a forceful personality, in his inevitable dealings with them, and kept up an impatient patter of insults that made the other boys feel he understood them through and through, as in a way he did. The thugs therefore respected him and left him alone, or if they gave him any trouble it was rather like cowardly dogs that will barrel into an attack from behind and at the last moment lose their nerve and skitter into the embankment; whereas the gentler boys worshipped him, as the type still do; and the stupid ones were in such awe of him that they kept their heads down at all times and left a yard or two of superstitious space between them and him if they could.

The thugs alone interested him, because he knew that he must by and by discover how not just to keep them in line but to enlist them fully to his purpose. The purpose itself was still nebulous, but nebulous in the manner of a volcanic cloud that drifts inexorably towards a bustling city, to wrap eventually all in its mighty embrace. The doctor sensed it too, and when the time came he directed the future supreme councillor to the handful of scholarships and bursaries then available to deserving youths in the provinces. They were mostly administered by the Army, and came mostly with a crippling lifelong obligation to that state within the state, whereby you signed over your whole existence to the Army in return for board and lodging and instruction at the elite academy, so-called. This did not greatly disturb the future supreme councillor, for whom in those days one life seemed as good as another, civilian or military, because he knew with a clarity that can have come neither from the murmuring forest nor the bright even light of the books—and least of all from the complacent monks—that whatever circumstances he would find himself in could be bent to his nebulous purpose by and by.

There was in those days, as there is still today, a certain higher justice in the way the bursaries were disbursed, and preference in the matter of scholarships was rarely given to the most deserving scholar. Rather, there was a more comprehensive principle at work, whereby factors such as the local prominence of the parents, or the assistance they were able to render those who administered the process, were taken into account, yet equally that preference was not set in stone but rather flowed like a merry brook in certain natural channels that could in their turn be diverted by those who had the wit and acumen to do so, and as a result a kind of fairness was after all ensured. And it was here that the doctor, for all his dreaminess and fumbling nature, came startlingly into his own. Because he in turn had benefited in his day from a bursary that set him on the scientific course, even though he had no aptitude whatever for the sciences, and he was therefore, and perhaps from his reading of popular fiction when nothing else was to hand, familiar with the workings of the system.

He forged testimonials with his own hand, the doctor, for he had in his youth shown an aptitude for drawing that grew into his lifelong love of art. He moved with great nimbleness between styles. He made calls on the telephone at times when the official in question was likely to be out of the office, and hinted to the underling that certain local or regional worthies had a great interest in the future supreme councillor's advance, to the elite academy. He did the voices with aplomb, silky or gruff, as the purpose might demand, and even aped some interference on the telephone line for good measure. There was a new spring in the doctor's step, and sometimes something like a giggle rose in his throat when he had delivered himself of one of these speeches. He got through to the elite academy itself, pretending to be one of the underlings with whom he had just conferred, and rendered them with such conviction that the future supreme councillor conceived a whole new respect for his mentor. And under some pretext he had a letter sent to him from a related agency in the capital—though not so directly relevant as to seem blatantly interfering—whose head and stamp he then patiently copied, over the course of several nights, to give the final push to the future supreme councillor's selection for the bursary.

The written exam and the *viva voce* were then mere formalities, though one of the examiners did point out, in a voice that trembled with patriotic fervour, or infirmity, that the youth had done the nation proud. Of this, it must in fairness be said, there had never been any doubt, because the youth was really as far as that went the ablest scholar of his generation, and miles ahead of any of the other candidates.

'Remember,' said the doctor when all was settled at last—it was the only advice for life he ever gave the future supreme councillor, and judging by its sententiousness must have come from one of the works they had read together early in their relationship— 'Remember,' the doctor said, and looked straight at him with his watery eyes, 'that the world is yours to shape, but if you make a dragon, you must pay for it.'

And so it was that one metallic, oddly blustery morning the youth boarded the bus at the clock tower, and heaved his bundle into the overhead net, and sat back in his seat, which smelt of oily hair and cigarette smoke, and closed his eyes, because he was then quite free of the sentimentality that has lately brought back his youth so much more vividly than he experienced it at the time. Off they set, in the squeaking, chuntering way the buses had then, and soon reached the junction with the dusty overland road, where with an enormous, bowel-deep crunch and clank the bus took its turn as though heaving itself on a new pair of railroad tracks, and he went to sleep with what he fully believes was the first smile of true contentment on his face.

15

With a hollow sputtering fart he comes to, as from a barrel. Is it a new day? Yet he lies in pitch darkness, and only the nocturnal animals can be heard in the gardens, and the muffled purr of a late motorcycle along the road. When this business is over he will have himself moved to the forest sanctuary in the hills, where a cool breeze swishes in the bamboo and large birds dance about the trees. Monkeys also, which are on the whole a manageable nuisance. In his old age he finds he derives a certain comfort from the distant monotonous chanting of the monks at dusk, for it is after all on their land that he has encroached, and it would not do to drive them away altogether. No, as long as they respect the boundaries—and being superstitious fools they respect them religiously—he has no objection to their mumbo-jumbo: it speaks of ancient rhythms and continuity, and it is at any rate better that people should believe in the old mumbo-jumbo than in nothing at all.

To think that the sanctuary had at one time been the scene of scandal! The head of the place of worship, whose honorific contained more long *ah*'s than any other name in history—it gave the supreme councillor great pleasure to utter it in company, just to watch the reaction of his audience: most assumed the requisite pious expression, the pursing of the mouth, the expectant blankness of the eyes, as the *ah*s careened out of his mouth like a freight train that never seems to want to end while you drum your fingers on the steering wheel at the crossing; but in the faces of one or two of his listeners he always detected a hint of the same hilarity the name inspired in him, expertly suppressed, and once or twice something like a sneer, which he came in time to regard as a dangerous sign —

The head of the place of worship was what the papers now call, with clumsy delicacy, *unusually rich*, and comported himself more and more in a manner unbefitting. Had it just been a question of the luxury cars, perhaps the villagers would have forgiven it; they by and large expect their betters to be conveyed in comfort. But the fellow started extorting bigger and bigger sums — and this from people who were already happy to part with a year's earnings and send their daughters to the city's whorehouses against the promise of a better fortune plus attendant rituals, from the place of worship; and to this day it has the spangly appearance of a carousel horse, quite out of keeping with the secluded location among the foliage. This is common enough in the provinces. What was worse was that the fellow, a square-set, bull-headed kind of brute, would then hector them about their other superstitions, for he was on top of everything else an adherent of the reformist branch, and keen to root out witchcraft and divining, other than that which he performed himself, at a premium, to say nothing of the amulets, and the shriving, which was something of a *specialite de la maison* in his day.

Well, you could not simply get rid of such a worthy, not then, and not now, nor was there, given the difficulty of the terrain, a viable alternative nearby, unless you had a jeep, which in those days were few. So the villagers by and by began to turn their backs when the fellow had himself driven about; they literally turned their backs on him, and stood gazing the other way or closely inspecting the wares or suddenly engrossed in conversation, until he was gone. On the morning rounds the monks found their routes deserted; and on the regular fast days and fetes there were by and by no longer any takers, and the grounds yawned from dawn till dusk, and the loudspeakers, lately installed at great expense to the flock, sat idle while their shadow crept across the beaten earth until it was swallowed by the woods. It being the nature of the arrangement that such things have to be provided by the community, the monks soon ran out of cleaning fluids and candles, and would have gone about hungry and dressed in rags had not the chief dug into his own ill-gotten holdings to buy supplies for them. And then one day the villagers struck the final blow.

It was the chief's habit, once or twice a week, to sequester himself in meditation in one of the sturdy steam baths or saunas they erect in the forest here, with two women who were neither young nor pretty, and there to remain for an hour or two until some shriving of the flesh had been satisfactorily performed; and when on the appointed day he had so sequestered himself, two of the bolder men, who were by profession woodcutters, or electricians, or had some other standing in the community, carried a great log to the hut and barred the exit. Once the hour was up, there could be heard— by those villagers who had concealed themselves in the vegetation, after issuing stern orders to their children to stay at home, on pain of a visit by the most vicious and irrational of the forest sprites—first a scraping and rattling, then a juddering, and a rumbling, and then a thrashing, but to no avail, for the old bath hut was sturdily built from great planks of hardwood and fortified with packed earth. Then the cries began, first the women, but soon the raspy voice of the abbot himself, first tentative, then commanding, then pleading, then fainter, and then nothing at all.

Only then did the villagers unblock the door, and they carried out the three sweat-drenched, grey-faced, naked bodies, and placed them carefully under an old banyan tree near the clearing, and dowsed them in cool water from the spring, and stood back in a small circle, for the first time in a long time facing the chief. Well, he came to by and by, and his mortification mingled with relief at finding himself still alive, and the villagers noted that the chief and one of the women had scraped their fingertips bloody and bruised their shoulders in the effort to get out of the stifling hut, but the other woman had barely any marks on her, and was dead.

Well, he became a very humble head after that, and ceased his preaching against the superstitions, and doled out the rituals and amulets to all comers for barely more than a nominal fee. His cars and land he donated to the community, except for one black large-finned limousine, which rusts on its blocks in one of the outbuildings to this day. And by and by, when he made his rounds on the back of an old pick-up truck, or increasingly on foot, the villagers prostrated themselves again, and fed the monks on their morning rounds, and made their donations, and when the fellow died, nearly two decades later, he had acquired the reputation of a holy man and was cremated with great honours and celebrated with a big party in the temple grounds, where the loudspeakers came fully into their own, one blaring out songs, the other prayers, and a third instructions to the crowd on such matters as parking and refreshments; and his spirit is now believed to inhabit the very same banyan tree in the clearing where he had been placed with his two women—only now the tree is twice the size it was then and wound around with ribbons, and a fresh glass of rice spirit is daily placed under it, and a slice of cake, and some fruit, and a banknote from the days before the currency reform, and only now and again does some wit add a tiny pair of lacy knickers, or an old bra, or a hubcap, to give the old ghost a taste of what he must surely be missing.

When what business is over? The supreme councillor has no sense of any pressing business except what the attendants whispered into his ear yesterday, or the day before, or at some other fairly recent time, and that did not seem particularly pressing. Its nature will presently come back to him. And yet the notion popped into his mind unbidden, that when this business is over he *will have himself moved into the forest*. And why this passivity? He might equally say that he *will move*, since the attendants and whichever conveyances they may command are in a way no more than extensions of his will— unconnected to his physical body, granted, but in another sense as much part of him as the toes, or more so, given that he has not seen his feet for many years, and thus perhaps more readily at his command.

He tended early to corpulence, perhaps as a result of the drastic improvement in diet when he moved to the elite academy, and with it into the highest circles of society, or else because it was always going to be his nature to be an enormous figure. He exercised in those days, with a kind of indolent vigour, and, while never presenting a particularly martial figure, he was well regarded by the instructors at the elite academy, who saw in him deep dormant resources of strength and a natural aptitude for command.

It was at the elite academy, too, that he formed the attachments that were to last for the rest of his life, with one or two of the fellow students there, who came from the greatest families in the land. He was not so unworldly as to be ignorant of their families, and yet unworldly enough to seek their company not for their provenance alone. He was also already so full—so bloated—with the sense of his own destiny that the sons of the great families were only ever going to become adjuncts or satellites of the great personage he was shaping up to be. In this they readily colluded, having cultivated a humility, in those final days of the feudal system, that was perhaps at some earlier point in history intended to be deceptive but had by then become part of their nature, so that they were easily overwhelmed by a forceful nature, provided they were given no other reason to disrespect it. And as the ablest scholar in the nation—

Yes, they formed lifelong bonds, in the classrooms and dormitories of the elite academy, and in the homes of some of the greatest families in the land. There he was soon made welcome, sometimes almost like an adopted son. This happened still in the last days of the feudal system, and to some extent happens even now, in one informal way or another, and many of the fathers, who had been educated at expensive schools abroad and read many of the books he had, and sometimes the mothers, were first tickled and then profoundly impressed by his ability to converse knowledgeably on a range of subjects, which often contrasted with their own humble—and, it has to be said, rather dull—sons'.

It was in many ways a less stratified society in those last feudal days, or perhaps the strata were at the same time more pronounced and more porous than they are now. Equally it is possible that he was simply a rare beast whom no stratum could contain and who was therefore able to move between them at will, despite his country accent, and his uncouth formal speech, and his poor clothes, in the initial stages. He readily allowed himself to be shaped by his new environment in these particulars, and soon spoke in the refined tones of the upper classes, if somewhat more forcefully and rapidly than they would have done, because he did not see how allowing himself to be so shaped would in any way diminish his immortal essence, nor how resisting it would further his nebulous aims. Few but the future supreme councillor in those days paid attention to the great political ideas that elevated uncouthness to a virtue in and of itself and had wreaked such profound havoc in the great advanced nations, and later the lesser too, so the question never arose.

His aims were slow to emerge from the mist, but it soon became clearer that they lay in the direction of leadership; whether he would exercise that leadership purely in the military field or wholly in the political sphere or somewhere between the two, if they could at all be separated, did not become evident until much later. Everyone, at any rate, predicted greatness for him, and wanted as it were a piece of him, be it out of curiosity, or opportunism, or some other more mixed motive, because it was clear that the feudal system was for the dustbin sooner rather than later, and it would be as well—so the fathers of his friends reasoned—to align oneself with the winning faction in the ensuing struggles. *Things must change*, as a great writer wrote, *so they can stay the same*. Yes, they practically vied for his affections, some of the greatest families in the land.

Some offered him their daughters. They must have had misgivings, but it was all done in the playful way with which people in this country so often mask their serious intent, even from themselves. It seems to the supreme councillor now that in deflecting these offers of advantageous marriage, kind or calculating as they may each in their different ways have been, casual or persistent, he got his first and most valuable lesson in practical politics. It took at times all his diplomacy and nerve to deflect them, and felt on occasion like talking a severely intoxicated man down from the electricity pylon from which he is determined to throw himself into the traffic. But not only did he not wish to offend them, he wished them afterwards to be as committed as they had hitherto been to furthering his career, and he wished to remain as welcome as before to their homes, of which he had become sincerely fond. He succeeded in almost every case, and turned only one of the families against him, where the daughter, or was it the mother—

All great leaders are solitary, no matter whether they marry or not, nor how many people they surround himself with. He made no absolute decision at the time; all he knew was that he must not marry *now*, though he might later, and it was only later that he became persuaded that he must not marry at all. As with so many things in his life he rather slipped into this perpetual bachelorhood. The reasons for it are not wholly clear to him, but about the rightness of the decision he has never had any doubt. He had a sense, if that is the way to describe it, that any attachment to a single partner, even strictly for show, would limit his range, both to himself and to the nation; it would set an indelible stamp on him, and he did not want to be stamped. Only lately has he begun to amuse himself with thoughts of going a-wooing, perhaps because the possibility no longer presents any threat to the actual state of affairs.

But now they want him to preside at a wedding: well, he may or may not, depending on the substance of the offer. The implications are vague so far, and committing himself to the role could in a way be as disastrous as getting married himself. Also it would interfere with his solitude, which despite the occasional visit from the attendants he feels is more complete now than it has ever been.

Even in the forest sanctuary in the hills he has never known true solitude. By the time he bought the mountain he was already so far advanced in public life that a retinue was inevitable, and it was not long before the people discovered his hideaway and the bolder and more determined among them made their laborious way up the tracks to petition him. Had he not instituted a rigorous regime whereby no company of any kind, except for the inevitable servants, was permitted after nine in the evening, he would have had no time to himself at all. It is only fortunate, he thinks, that he has always favoured his own company, for neither in front of a crowd of thousands nor on this vast solitary wedding bed need he ever be without it.

16.

'Fight, fight!'

'We stand behind you! No, Elder Brother—Elder Brother no: we stand *beside* you.'

'The nation stands beside you.'

'The nation!' The man is in tears. 'I love the nation.'

'You are all very kind.'

The minister has had to acquire a manner for convivial occasions with the years; he is not a naturally convivial man. Spending most of his career among thugs has helped a great deal, acquainting him with the narrow channels into which this not naturally expressive nation shunt their expressiveness, when drunk. This usually takes the form of growing insistence on ever fewer points of interest, so that by the final stage they may simply utter a harsh, inarticulate, insistent cry, over and over and over, having forgotten everything but the insistence itself, before that too is forgotten and they pass out head-first on the table. They go through a number of distinct stages before that, such as lewdness and maudlin patriotism, usually in that order, as though harrying each sentiment for what riches of hot satisfaction it might yield and, having found it yielded none, or sucked it dry, discarding it like a crab shell.

In his student days he was deeply uncomfortable in the presence of these histrionics, and the thugs, like dogs, could smell it through the fumes of their inebriation, and would set on him like dogs, and might once or twice have done him actual bodily harm had not their drunkenness rendered them too sluggish for the trim, young, nimble future minister. It was then, he thinks, what it is now: *metabolism*.

In the long run, however, flight was not the answer. He must needs come to some kind of arrangement with conviviality. Pretending did not work: he had tried for example to join in with their songs or their toasts, but something had betrayed him—the stiff spine, the strained eyes—and they had only mocked him more savagely and set on him again. So if he could not fully join them nor turn his back, it remained to try a kind of benevolent indifference, a smile as wholly without condescension as he could make it, and as modest and free of judgement, yet not obsequious either, but distant, apart, so as to present no target within reach of the thugs. All it required of him was patience and a saintly endurance of boredom, which he found in the ancient practice of meditation and the routine of the police procedural. If he ever threatened to snap, he recited to himself a mantra, silently in his head, or imagined transcribing a witness statement concerning the evening so far, in triplicate, and taking it for signature to the superior officer, who was engaged on other business.

This strategy was at last successful, and thereafter the worst that ever came to him from the thugs was a little light banter concerning his temperance, which was borne of respect more than anything else, and helped rather than hindered his growing authority as he rose through the ranks. More, it had the paradoxical effect of freeing him every now and again to enjoy one of these drinking sessions, where every fresh glass he consented to share drew fresh cheers from his boon companions, so called, and of spurring them to solicitude if he ever got badly drunk.

So much of politics, the minister thinks, depends on the acquisition of certain defensive skills, on the ability to keep your fellow men at bay, rather than on your convictions or even, as the popular wisdom has it, connections. A charismatic man like his friend the superintendent need of course never move at all, and can silence the most inebriated thug with the force of his still presence alone; but if you have no charisma you are just as well off with a handful of these strategies, since a powerful man is one who seems to make no great bid for the approval of others but instead gives the impression that it is his approval that they must seek.

Tonight, too, the minister has smiled modestly and distantly, and allowed himself to be the still centre around which a great deal of commotion has tended to swirl without quite touching him. He has a vague sense of magnetic forces, negative charges, something about friction and the absence thereof, but science is not his field. Perhaps he means ball bearings. He at any rate perceives himself as the axle or axis around which by some mechanical trick these forces have been persuaded to turn, shepherded—propelled?—by his friend the superintendent. Toasts were raised. Appeals were launched. By the end of the evening there was something like conviction in the stale air, among this inner circle of thugs and semi-thugs.

The notion came to him, as they cheered and shouted and stuffed themselves with the never-ending parade of dishes, at what he very much fears is his own expense, that a smoking ban in all restaurants or enclosed convivial spaces may well be one way of ensuring the needed final push of support among the virtuous voting crowd. That, however, would require close consultation with Health, who is a jelly-like nonentity and lackey of the Leader's, so the measure may have to wait until his replacement after the minister's ascent. Or a clash could be engineered, whereby the jelly—

The feeling in general—they call him *elder brother* as convention demands, and indeed are mostly his juniors by anything between a year and a decade, so their appeals for all their force have a wheedling quality— The feeling in general, among the inner circle, is that his chances are rather better

136

than he at first anticipated, and that sources of funding are popping up all over the place. At the same time, little can be read into the atmosphere of mindless boosterism that always surrounds any hope and ambition in this country, because to douse the flames of enthusiasm with the cold water of reason would be considered inexcusably rude, especially if the ambition is your host's.

Yes, they all want him to challenge, the thugs and semi-thugs with the excellent connections, in the military and the force and the bureaucracy, in business and finance. But they may believe that that is what he wants to hear, and one must further allow, in this country, for the fervour with which a drunk man may express both one view and its opposite, on alternate evenings, depending on the company he keeps. The minister has listened keenly for false notes, especially among the more reliable members of the inner circle. The semi-thug in finance, who for some reason managed to hold on to much of his holdings in the last economic calamity, despite the dubious ways in which he came by and managed them, to the point where no small part of the calamity must in fact be attributed to him and his ilk—

The semi-thug in finance seemed even more certain of their success than the others, and performed on a napkin a swift, deft calculation that was all the more persuasive for having the air of a three-card trick, and was much applauded by everyone.

Still, the minister has thought it wise to detain his friend the superintendent into this hour of mild regret and ebbing spirits, here among the detritus of their meal, in the murky, cavernous interior of their favourite restaurant. To compare notes, pick over the remains; to subject them to sobering reflection. And here they sit, their chairs at three o'clock around their favourite round table, savouring the silence, permitting their heavy limbs to sink more comfortably into the ballroom chairs.

He is in no hurry to break the silence, that too is a trick he has learnt in the years of active service. The superintendent is in no hurry either, having still more years of active service under his ever-widening belt. Well, this is not a contest: they have all the time in the world.

At last the superintendent says, 'The suit—'

'Yes,' says the minister. 'That occurred to me too.'

'Has it been twenty years?'

'Nearer twenty-five.'

'And a bad fit from Day One.'

'When was Day One?'

'Ah—' The superintendent chuckles, because the ancient maître d', or whatever his designation is, may have been working in this place long before they ever set foot in it, may have been working here since the beginning of time, with his dreadful servility, his lolloping gait, his greasy old ill-fitting suit. But every other member of staff has been replaced a thousand times: they are little generic youngsters from the provinces, with an air of utter terror that is no doubt part of their job description and in no way reflects their true mental state.

The maître d' stands in the depths of the *salle* now, barely visible by the kitchen door, misshapen in the celebrated suit, like a guard at the back entrance to the underworld.

'That man,' says the superintendent, 'must be privy to more secrets and intrigue than anyone else in the land, except perhaps the supreme councillor himself.'

'Perhaps he is his eyes and ears.'

'Or very rich. There was at one time a rumour that his daughter was studying at some elite university abroad, or studies there still.'

'Yes, still: I heard it first a decade or more ago, and it seems only last week—'

They reflect for a moment on the possibilities.

―――

'If he reports back—'

'Then he is no use to anyone, and would long be gone. Or else he reports on everyone to everyone.'

'He has never reported to me.'

'Nor me.'

The superintendent leans forward. 'Is that even the same man?'

'There is a fellow haunts the meat counter in the supermarket where my wife shops—'

'Used to shop.'

'Oh no, she still shops.'

The superintendent raises his eyebrows. 'There is another point in your favour.'

The minister does not see it. 'The Leader's wife shops. She does nothing else.'

'I do not mean luxury handbags, under escort. Groceries.'

'Ah.'

'The proximity to the—'

'Yes-yes. All these things can play either way. It is the calculations I am more interested in.'

'Has he—?' The superintendent looks around the table for the napkin.

'No, he pocketed it.'

'Ah.'

'The calculations in general; the numbers. Do you believe them?'

'I have no reason not to.'

'Is that the same thing?'

The superintendent laughs. 'It is in my line of work: we look for the acceptable truth, the plausible explanation. Or no, we look for the least implausible one.'

'We look for a reason not to believe.'

'Yes, and when we find none—'

'—then we take the statement, in triplicate.'

'Exactly.'

'Then I rephrase my question: do these numbers, these calculations, carry to your mind enough force—never mind how true or untrue—to mow down all doubt before them? We are not here to persuade a judge, this is—'

'Oh, much bigger, yes, but the principle is the same.'

'I am talking about force. Immense force, in view of the immense force stacked against us.'

'I think you have given the answer,' says the superintendent, and leans heavily back in his chair. 'Stacked against us, you said. Us. You have already decided.'

The minister's expression does not change.

'All we have is assurances, promises, undertakings, plus great drunken enthusiastic claims of a groundswell in the hinterland, whatever that means. All this will need to be parlayed into an impression of enormous popular will. Of power, before we have it.'

'That is very good,' says the superintendent, looking ever more pleased. 'Power before we have it. There is your task.'

'So?'

'My view?'

'As my oldest friend.'

'You know I am here to persuade you?'

'Even so.'

The superintendent sighs. Finally he says: 'Fifty-fifty.'

The minister peers at him through the murk.

'At best.'

'Thank you.' The minister relaxes in his ballroom chair. 'In a certain light the chances are at best fifty-fifty in any plausible contest. In that event the question merely becomes—'

'—what tips it?'

'Yes.'

'Three strikes. Something the current administration will be incapable of carrying out. Each as you say *of a different flavour*.'

The superintendent leans forward again. 'You have something?'

'I may,' says the minister modestly, 'have a few ideas. It will require delicate handling, and at any rate I would rather not force it. We must first make sure of broad support. The last thing we need is upheaval. We stand'—he means himself—'for stability. We stand for the firm hand, but the steady hand. Ours is not the swift blow, or the iron fist. Ours'—he takes a drink from his replenished glass—'is the guarantee that the last year-and-a-half of bold innovation have been more than a flash in the pan. We fortify. We consolidate. We steer a steady course. Or else—'

'Yes,' says the superintendent. 'I do not see what other line you could take.'

The minister snuffles. 'We shall have to flatter him out of office.'

'Reports of erratic behaviour.'

'Exhaustion.'

'Burnout.'

The minister raises a hand. 'All that, to be carefully handled. These people are not idiots. All we really have is an appearance of preternatural calm. Have you ever seen a tsunami?'

'Thankfully, no.' The superintendent probably has business interests in coastal areas, no doubt related to the encroachment of tourist operations on the national parks.

'I saw a film once, at a conference under the aegis— A tsunami is the calmest spectacle in the world. It is merely a long slow wave coming in, inexorably. In, and in, and in. Along the way it may uproot trees and tear up houses, but from a certain vantage they are of no consequence. A vast expanse of calm water calmly moving: that is the impression, no matter what havoc it may be wreaking on the way. It is a restful sight, from a certain vantage. Reassuring. It is

---

141

conceivable that people would simply stand there and let it come, this great calm that comes at them. On the other hand—'

'—they might run.'

'Quite. We can afford no focus, is my point, on the agitation. The trees. The houses—'

The superintendent nods, satisfied. 'You have decided for some time.'

'Decided? No. The decision was made for me.' The minister knuckles the table with his fist. 'I have no choice.'

'Good,' says the superintendent. 'I like that. It is good.' He leans forward on his hams and stretches his arms. 'And now it is late.'

'Yes.' The minister is already on his feet. 'You must go home to your wife, and I to mine. They will be—'

'—impatient.'

17

Nothing from the slum, for days now. The supreme councillor has circled and circled, in his fitful old-man's dreams, in the approximate area where he believes it located, and nothing. But between searching in vain for the woman, he has seen glorious things elsewhere. Oh, beautiful: in the noonday glare beyond the city limits, a man climbing, climbing one of the skeletal poles that hold up hoardings across eight or ten lanes of traffic: a man stripped to the waist, rail-thin, grey-complexioned and sweating, but intent, intent, and all the while screaming in a steady tearing rasp, like an animal in fury at its pain; climbing first the skeletal pole, then on reaching the knee creeping slowly, unsteadily across the intolerable glare of the road below, freeing now one hand, now the other, to shake it furiously at the indifferent traffic— Already the spectators assemble, staring blankly up at the sight, the way people stare here, witnesses without investment, the women sheltering their faces with documents or newspapers against the noonday sun, and the distant siren whooping—

How unimportant he looks there, among the gleams of watery sunlight in the aluminium struts. The story? Oh, the story is always the same, a broken heart, or empty pockets, and more usually both, his woman shacked up with another man, perhaps a police officer with a steadier income, or a steadier hand. All night he will have sat cross-legged in his hut, smoking from his foil, ranting to himself, first under his breath, then louder, disturbing the peace. Inevitably by and by other voices were raised, till he ran and ran, in a heat of speed, and now he has gone to put an end to the intolerable pain, in the eight or ten lanes of traffic. But he waits too long or creeps too slowly, the authorities arrive, the articulated crane, the tensed tarpaulin to halt his fall, and soon also the press; and the crowd mills below and the loudhailer drowns out his screams—

These crises galvanise a community, and are in a sense a blessing, because after great commotion the collective instinct is to be roughly kind to the cause of the disturbance, and help him roughly on his way; perhaps he will not do it again and go back where he came from, chastened, to the gentler grind of forest or plain.

The city is not for everyone, the supreme councillor reflected as he moved on to the next wonder, and the outskirts cruellest of all, with their immense empty distances, as if something had gone wrong with time and space, so that you walk and walk for half an hour or more and still you have gained but a fraction of the distance to the next crossing, and nothing but the towers of tyres still in the vast weedy lot at your side—

Still, for those who can bear it or do not see, what opportunities! There, along the half-paved back road, a fat woman perched on a high stool, amid corrugated siding. A blackish puddle at her feet from the last rain, a smell of engine grease in the air, and in her right hand the arm of a kind of one-armed bandit, and a translucent sack of tin cans by her side. A taste of iron on her tongue. Though she is fat she works the lever with beady enthusiasm, with a sporting relish of attack. Passers-by shout encouragement, ironically or not, who knows? The fellow who bums cigarettes, with his stupid-sly squint and his poor wisps of facial hair, the landlord's floozy, the old bat who does the manicures and invariably cuts too close to the quick and draws blood— There she sits, the fat woman, intent on her task, for which they pay her a pittance.

She is what they call an economic refugee, from a neighbouring country. Her hips are something to behold, bulging over the stool: at least she has enough to eat, here, and a task to occupy her. One of those fortunate natures who take pleasure in little things, and greet each new day with fresh enthusiasm.

A kilo done, she slides heavily off the stool, stretches her arms over her head, which results in a mountainous bunching of flesh and fabric at her front, and sways across the track, to the polished pebble-dash table and matching benches that do duty, here, as a hearth. Two tarry grilled fish are laid out there, on rolled-back plastic bags, white flesh bursting from the splits, beside some muddy salad in a plastic bowl, for everyone to help themselves. She pours water from a little bottle over her hands, wipes them on her t-shirt and tucks in, with the same relish she brings to her work. Chewing, she smiles.

These are the scenes that gladden the supreme councillor's golden heart. What she is making, from the tins, with the old one-armed press, are little washers that hold down roofing panels on sheds and barns and houses, sold by the kilo, a modest but vital supply, without which our roofs would fly clean away in a storm. And if it puts food in the mouth of a woman who loves her food, any food, perhaps because the memory of hunger still gnaws, or because she comes easily to pleasure: why, is that not in a way the best industry of all?

This inclination to sentimentality, to rising sob and trembling lip at the drop of a hat, is a function of the supreme councillor's extreme old age and has opened up, so late in the day, a whole new gambolling ground of sensual pleasure for him. Oh, beautiful: the flappy loosening of tension in the upper chest, as of a stiff rag being shaken free, or a piece of siding rattling in the wind, and in the eyes a prickle of cleansing fluid— You are never too old, he thinks, to discover

145

new aspects of our boundless animal nature. The impatience of his youth, on the other hand, where has that gone? The brisk long strides with which he marshalled enormous forces, the irritability? How he harangued the poor old monk in the clearing! All subsumed, that is his feeling, into the long view he has long taken of human affairs. Perhaps he has not always suffered fools gladly, but he suffers them gladly now, and they are in a sense his favourites: on fools he smiles, and now it is the smart people he despises— Or no, he despises no one now, but he can see all their folly bared to the noonday sun.

And yet, how these emotions tend at the last to an odder reaction still, a sobbing giggle that makes the jowls judder and the belly quiver and fat tears course down into the ticklish old ears, where they dry, a mild freshening irritation, like dewdrops.

Also he has seen: an overloaded boat, sinking; a lunatic, defacing an idol and beaten swiftly to death by the pious crowd; belief, the importance of; an old woman hoarding rubbish and cats, so that no room remains for her in her three-storey house but a few narrow walkways among the stinking bags and her filthy bed, from which she rises each morning to resume her weary tasks, of hoarding rubbish and cats; a vast foreign car, driven into a crowd; a pickpocket, tricked out as pickpocket, with sidling gait and devious mien, coming up fast behind people and swerving at the last moment away; the essential childishness of this nation; a policeman, shooting his gun sideways into the head of an economic refugee from a neighbouring country, or an insurgent, the whole thing is over so fast it is hard to tell; a descendant of one of the old families, filling sheet after sheet of paper with tiny drawings; a descendant of an old family, driving his vast foreign car into a young couple; the extraordinary resourcefulness of this nation; a doctor, tying the chopped-up remains of his wife into neat parcels and stuffing them down a storm drain; the swift, perfunctory couplings of the young; the blank faces of the rich; starched silks, starched silks—

And furthermore this: an enormous commerce of people, pouring like water over the escalators and onto the concourse below, swirling, eddying, then marshalled in enormous numbers, processed, stamped, badged, corralled, moved, seated in hushed, reverent anticipation, lifted, flung— And tireless industry, and the immense trembling flow of the arterial roads, so that, from a certain vantage, all is order, serenity, beauty, and from another all disorder and madness, and *competence* and *efficiency*, the great prizes of the present world order, merely a question of the appropriate distance from the object, so that the question should be less *in what way is this different or similar to what I expect of it*? than *what is it trying to achieve*? This body that moves, this motion: does it serve its own purpose if it does not serve mine? Is there a better purpose, all things considered and being equal, to which it should be made to move? And if not, can I resign myself to its purpose, can I sink into it, as one sinks into soft pillows on a vast wedding bed? Will it swallow me whole and extinguish me? And if so, what argument can I raise against my extinction?

And he has seen the vast grief of a plain illiterate woman, in an outsize t-shirt, at her husband's elopement, after thirty years of marriage, with a floozy from the nearby tenements, and her pilgrimage, every late afternoon thereafter, to the side of the great arterial road, in sure expectation of his return, for all would then be forgiven—

147

But the woman with the boil has vanished. His favourite. Well, you reach the limits of your powers sooner than you would hope, and while the nation can properly speaking have no secrets from him, any one individual may yet escape his eagle eye for days, or weeks, or months on end. Years perhaps, who is to say? There remains, however, the intuition—the all-but-certainty—that his unconscious powers of oversight are greater still than his conscious ones, and that those who cannot for the moment be accounted for are by definition those who are up to nothing of any great interest, and face no great threat, and are therefore on both counts safe. That this intuition can never, by definition, turn into full certainty, does not bother him greatly: there comes a time when a man must learn to trust his intuitions or give up altogether. What the supreme councillor does not know is not worth knowing, of that he is all but certain—which is why they gave him, on retirement, the title he now holds.

There is no Supreme Council, nor are there any other supreme councillors, far less any ultimate authority he might advise. But on casting around, on his retirement, for a title to distinguish him above all other men in the nation, so that even on retirement from active service he might legitimately tower or loom over them, the government of the time had recourse to this curious vestige of the feudal era; which would make no sense except that there had long been a feeling abroad that he was *supreme* in his knowledge of the higher secrets, and the lesser workings, and would put his insight at the disposal, in an advisory or *counselling* capacity, to those ostensibly in charge; and it was with some relief that, after floating a few self-evident duds, such as *minister mentor*, they alighted on the honorific, or title, by which he is now known to every last man Jack and woman Jill in the land, even if they can no longer recall—as he for the moment cannot—his proper name.

He knew at an early age that the time would come when he could no longer recall his own name, since his enormous mental capacity has always been deficient in this one particular, that he could never remember names. It has to do, he thinks, with a lack of filial attachment, or perhaps an inherited trait, or mineral deficiency in some part of the brain, owing to nutrition or some such cause, and has manifested itself from an early age in a curious buzzing noise in his ears whenever he was introduced to anyone by name. In his maturity it would take him anywhere between several weeks and several months to learn anyone's name, even those of his closest advisors, and then only when he had seen it written down, and even so it was apt to slip his mind at the slightest provocation— Thankfully he soon reached a position where he no longer needed to remember people's names, or where at least they were no longer in a position to take offence if he did not, and at any rate the enormous capacity of his memory allowed him to identify them without fail by other characteristics, such as the face, or the history, or the gait, or the stench—

In this deficiency, too, he is at odds with the nation he supposedly embodies and whose uncanny knack for remembering names for months, or years, after a single introduction, strikes him as essentially of the Third World, as the manifestation of an essentially oral culture. That that is the nature of this culture does not embarrass him, as it does some of the younger generation of leaders, educated as they still are abroad. It is merely the case. He is part of this culture even as he divagates from it, with his vast reading. Truth be told he has barely read more than a few hundred books since he came of age. Their deadness, compared to the living, throbbing, wiggling liveliness of life— Make that a thousand or two, who knows? The point is well made, that he is the stuff of legend, transubstantiated in the spoken, not the written, word, the title whispered in awe: *the supreme councillor.*

18.

For the first time the minister's support rating is ahead of the Leader's, in the monthly poll by a university. This must have come to the Leader's attention. How could it not? A man so jealous of every drop of what may, at a stretch, be interpreted as the love of his people probably feels these sloshings in his water. The minster remembers seeing a display in the window of some shop or office in which a clear tank of viscous blue liquid tipped slowly, inexorably from side to side, to simulate the movement of waves; what can it have been trying to advertise? Something like it, at any rate, he imagines exists in every politician's mind.

But did the latest figures cast a pall over the morning's Cabinet meeting? It was in many ways the usual monologue. Foreign Affairs, once the press had been ushered out and the monologue got underway, went softly to sleep, then woke and excused himself, not to be seen again. The rest of them sat there, in the usual rictus of boredom, at the long blond laminated conference table. Finance looked ever further down his long nose, except when, every now and again, he lifted both cupped hands, as from the depths of a clear pool, and smoothed back the magnificent coiffure. He emerged from these self-ministrations chin-first, refreshed. Did or did not Sports play a computer game, under the conference table? His face gave nothing away, only the occasional microscopic tilt of a shoulder and stiffening of the neck suggested that he was responding to stimuli other than the Leader's flow of promises, announcements, pledges, schemes, threats, harangues, maunderings, meanderings and general verbal excreta of one kind or another as they slowly rose all about them and smothered the room.

The stench— Lately the minister has had a feeling that it is a physical manifestation of some imbalance in the Leader's humours, a sour metallic smell, as of oiled gunmetal, that emanates barely noticeably from his sphincter of a mouth, the row of small, tight, pointed teeth. Or the minister's mind is playing tricks, manifesting a sense that hangs about the Leader of waste products ill digested, of toxins uncleansed, which corresponds to the waxy deadness of his skin, its high ill sheen. What does he take to keep him on edge? Presumably something prescribed—

Thoughts like these kept the minister occupied; also the discreet browsing of documents. Perhaps there was nothing particularly jittery about the Leader's performance, and it was only an awareness heightened by the minister's own plotting that made it seem to him that the words *social order* rang out thin, high and metallic more than once over the bowed heads of the Cabinet, like lashes with a length of wire. Perhaps there was no uncommon focus on *policing* to the torrent of words, given the Leader's own background in the force, if indeed there was any focus at all. And yet he could have sworn that it was at the words *social order* that Foreign Affairs came to, with a discreet smack of the lips, and remembered his prior engagement.

Culture by contrast was unable to settle down, though she is normally a great one for snoozing. This is not decisive evidence—perhaps she had eaten something that did not agree with her; though again the minister has a notion that there are very few victuals that do not agree with Culture— She shifted in her chair, and at one point dropped the magazine and struggled heartbreakingly to retrieve it from under the table without attracting notice, which for some reason directed the Leader's ire at Agriculture and Fisheries, than whom he has no more loyal ally and who, though only a few years younger, calls the Leader 'father' —

Strange, the man's sensitivity in these matters: his fury is always somehow redirected, dissipated; he would never lash out straight at Culture for dropping her magazine, or for reading it in the first place during his perorations, yet at the same time the true object of it is always stingingly clear to everyone — or everyone but Agriculture and Fisheries, who cringed like a whipped dog. There perhaps is the true love the Leader craves, and of course he disdains what he can have.

No, it was a fraught Cabinet meeting, all in all. Its tenor, or rather the tenor of its tenor, was perhaps perceptible only by the shy cutting of the hooded baby eyes every now and again in the minister's direction, when it might have seemed that the minister was not looking —

And then, just once, their eyes met.

It was certainly, he admits to himself, an experience, to find himself caught in the full force of the great baby eyes, with the hoods for once all the way up. The gaping void. For a second it seemed to the minister as if the Leader kept this especial horror in reserve for his enemies, that he let them glimpse the gaping void behind the eyes. Did the minister's own eyes widen in shock? He hopes and trusts not, what with the years of staring down suspects; he hopes and trusts he maintained a reptilian inscrutability. But he is not at all sure that he could have borne it much longer, teetering there on the edge of the void. Yes, he might easily have caved in and looked away, had not Culture at that moment dropped her magazine, with a rustle and a little sigh that sounded, of all things, like muted sexual ecstasy. Perhaps the fury the Leader took out on poor Agriculture was really at having certain victory in the staring contest snatched from him at the last moment —

Then again, everyone knows not to catch the eye of madmen and drunks. Perhaps the minister simply made a mistake he had never made before and stared at the man, who was as surprised as he was.

Be that as it may, something passed between them; and now, by accident or appointment, the Leader seems to be moving in on the minister's turf, of *social order* and *policing*, and a line will have to be drawn, fences erected, trenches dug, guns emplaced; because once the Leader moves onto any turf he leaves nothing but scorched earth behind. Were Agriculture, for instance, not such a faithful hound, he would long have despaired of the promises: the land reform, the free seeds, and to every farmer a cow— No, though the lines have been drawn sooner than the minister would have hoped, it is as well for them to be drawn now, when he is still freshly energised by his purpose. So what if time is short? There is never enough of time, and always too much of it: it is how a man negotiates the available quantities that counts.

In the chill privacy of the ministerial van, he makes calls, on a telephone registered to the gardener's wife. The subterfuge serves a higher purpose, of subverting the subterfuge of those who must even now be busy starting to encircle him. That is what it will come down to in the end, the question of who runs the tighter rings around the other.

'Developments,' says the voice on the other end.

'Good?'

'Oh, all good, commitments—'

'To the tune of?'

'That is what I asked.' The oiled chuckle rattles for a moment over the ether in chopped-up parcels, which remind the minister obscurely of the evening muster of his time in the force, the serried ranks. Really, for all his so-called prowess in the communication field, the Leader's systems are rarely as reliable as one might wish.

There is a salty saying in the language that describes these triumphs of appearance over substance, there always is. Perhaps all languages have a roughly equal store of sayings — who would count the stars in the sky? But it seems to the minister that speakers of all classes in this country pepper their speech more liberally with them than elsewhere, perhaps due to the dearth of elevated oratory or literary reference. No one more than three generations from farmers: hence the homely associations, the spurious levelling effect.

And yet, people from one street to the next may purport never to have heard the proverbs that you take for granted, so that they might as well be made up one and all, and anyone with the knack could simply invent his own and attribute them to the proverbial grandmother. There is, as you would expect, a preponderance of agricultural metaphors, and culinary wisdom, and an endless store related to domestic or farmyard animals, and a smattering of mythical creatures. Never park the boat against the stream. Wait to cut the bamboo until you see the water. Beware of the ducks — what can that ever have been trying to say? All no doubt nonsense.

'Well?'

'They gave me to understand the war chest was practically —'

The ministerial van rocks up a motorway ramp, and for a moment there is nothing but what in the old analogue days would have been called static.

'I lost you for a moment. Was practically what?'

'Unlimited.'

'My god, they must —'

'Yes, we knew that. But it is good to have these assurances sealed, stamped and in the drawer.'

155

'They hardly gave them sealed and stamped.'

'A turn of phrase. They are at any rate committed.'

'So?'

'It will be enough.'

'It has to be. But on the question of the public relations firm—'

'—not to be won over. We were able to put out only the most tentative feelers, and they are if anything even more committed to *his* cause, being part-owned by an entity—'

'There is a surprise. My question was rather whether anything remotely approaching their prowess can be found anywhere else in this sorry country.'

There is a belief abroad that—more still than the promises and the up-front largesse and the backing of huge parts of the financial sector—what won the last election was simply the vastly superior quality of the election posters, in the national colours, with their simple, modern, televisual clarity. The minister is inclined to dismiss that as an advertiser's fantasy, but it is true that the images of all candidates in sharp haircuts, neckties and blousons of a reassuring corporate navy, for example, stood out enormously against the fat, heavily retouched faces of the other parties, in their white fantasy uniforms, with their amateurish fading effects into a yellowish or pinkish dawn, to say nothing of the foolish ornate fonts. Thus too were the press releases written, the reporters briefed, the public appearances orchestrated: sleekly, sharply. Some such operation will be greatly needed if the overthrow is to succeed.

'We may have to look overseas, there is no one that we have spoken to who seemed even remotely—'

'Remotely what?'

'*Professional*, if that is the word—'

'That is the word all right. But no, out of the question. We would lay ourselves wide open to allegations of treason. No.

We may have to trust to the appeal of a certain comfortable incompetence, a blundering familiarity, a return to the—'

A silence at the end of the line.

'Are we cut off again?'

'I am thinking.'

'I did not mean *that* degree of blundering familiarity,' the minister snaps. He sits up. 'No, forgive me, we need all the thinking we are capable of, at any time of the day or night. So. Can we pull these strands together?'

'The strands being?'

'In fact,' continues the minister at the same rapid clip, 'I was quite wrong to complain. I rely enormously on your thinking, by some distance the sharpest I have encountered, as witness the esteem in which you are held—'

His friend laughs. 'No, no, you have a—force I have not seen since our youth. This is all for the good. The *strands* you mention being, on the one hand, a continuation of the modernising efforts set in train by this government, and on the other hand, a return to the continuity that has served this nation—'

'That is the message, yes.'

'All of everything.'

'No, the stress on continuity in innovation, innovative continuity, dependable reform, modern conservatism, conservative modernity, in whatever wording resonates among the peasantry and the aspiring urban classes, winking as it were over the heads of one at the other, or vice versa.'

'If you had not gone into politics you would have made a great advertiser.'

'Yes-yes,' says the minister, bored now with the banter. 'They can at least manage that, no? Whichever lot we employ?'

'We must hope so.'

'We must do better, we must *make* them.' He balls a knuckly fist. 'Keep them on the tightest possible leash, threaten them

---

157

with the full weight of the law, according to any interpretation I shall wish to put on it, make them quake in their soft shoes and lie awake in their vulgar condominiums, next to their doctored wives, and grind their orthodontics in their fitful sleep, when at last it comes—'

'Oh yes, you are on fire—'

'Well, we shall have to concentrate, is my point. The camp must be reinforced, the watches doubled, the time is nearly at hand—'

'I am concentrating as we speak.'

19.

They are up to their old tricks again, the supreme councillor has suspected it for some time. No sooner do you turn your back than they are up to their old tricks. He sighs in his sleep. It is for this reason that his back is never really turned; he is a weathervane, barring the evident dissimilarities: a golden weathervane of enormous girth. Perhaps some such likeness could be manufactured commercially and sold in the gift shop, once the aurification is complete in a century or two. And never any rest for the magnificent mind, even in his deepest sleep.

Always plotting, this unruly nation, yet never planning, that is why they need the guiding hand: they live for the day but desire the overthrow of the peaceful system by tomorrow morning, for no better reason than that they are bored. Well, not on his watch; not while he still draws breath. They would regret it bitterly if it came, the overthrow, and mourn the peaceful system till the end of time. All spirit would go out of them. It is in their own best interest that things should stay, within reason, the same, change though they inevitably must. The answer is to offer them no solid surface to direct their flailing blows against. Hence the weather-vaning, the pivoting, the slow graceful pirouetting that he has performed for uncountable years, first in active service, then in active retirement, and at long last here on his wedding bed. Also to avoid bed sores. He chuckles in his sleep. Yes, they are up to their old tricks again, he can see them at it now.

One of them is at the long game, he can see him now, yet impatient with it, that is the curious thing. There is a whiff of— a whiff of— No, the supreme councillor cannot put his finger on it: a sour metallic taste, something curdled, something ingrown and stale, and a terrible gaping void where one might suppose the sense to be located. Oh, beautiful: how the fellow has turned all these disadvantages to advantage, the lack of wit, the want of charm, the want, the want—

Now he grants wishes. Is that not ever the mark of greatness? Now he is a benefactor. Wherever he goes, people approach him with their needs and wants, and it is through their needs and wants that he understands them. The supreme councillor chuckles, and shakes an imaginary fat forefinger at him, in his sleep. Oh yes, he is at the long game, that one, he would first buy the nation then turn it into a docile workforce for his kraken of enterprises, in one way or another. How petitioner and petitioned are ever cut from the same cloth, and one answers the needs and wants of the other. Prick up your ears, and the call ever comes back like an echo, your wants, their needs, your needs, their wants— Their ambitions are so monotonous: to win the lottery, to run the country, to steal the nation's wealth, to encroach on protected land. A television, a mobile phone, a small restaurant. Or else to grow trees for the paper mill and never work again another day. Or as might be love, if that is in short supply—

So he schemes, that one, and plots and plans, with the aid of his wife, who is the brains behind the operation; her presence overlays the sour bass note with a heady stench of wax blossom. They are up to something large and looming, he can see them at it now, though there is an air about the two of them, in their bathroom slippers, in the marble-floored drawing room, that makes him pull back involuntarily— Perhaps it will be enough to press to the wall, so to speak, one of his vast pink pendulous ears, with the hairs sprouting freely from the cavities. The pair of them are readying themselves to strike a decisive blow, you can tell from the strain in their voices, their avid breathing. They are about the business of crushing an enemy, who in turn— No, not one enemy, two, or perhaps enemy is the wrong word; the right word for the moment escapes the supreme councillor. But a fiendish plan. He wags his imaginary forefinger at them.

They seem to command impressive surveillance equipment. Mechanical, of course, since they lack the supreme councillor's gift, and with all the problems mechanical equipment brings: no matter how it purrs, in the final analysis it cranks and clanks, it rattles, sputters and creaks, and has none of his ease or range. Even so, impressive. They know the enemy's movements all right, nothing much escapes them. They plot and plan, and under their avid hands a course of action takes shape. Three strikes—

Also their powers of calculation. The supreme councillor shudders. The reflex carries the atavistic memory of a dog shaking its fur clean of wetness, of contamination.

But the central figure in this drama, if it can be called that— and the supreme councillor has frankly heard more amusing stories in his time—is the other one. Now that is an altogether more congenial figure, for all that he is a thin, dry, charmless stick of a man, order, order, order all the hours that God sends, and the documents in triplicate. Still, one warms involuntarily to the fellow, it is hard to say how or why. He has that charm which is given by a higher power to the charmless who do not care about charm.

See how intently he is about his business, how single-mindedly. See how keenly his lean, sharp, narrow mind fillets the available information. Also how he wrestles with his conscience, or it with him; how he has emboldened himself. He works the phones, tirelessly. He is on to the Leader's excellent surveillance equipment, and has managed to bypass some of it. He has had his office discreetly swept, and the phones he uses are registered to innocent third parties. The meetings take place in his usual haunts, to give no impression that anything out of the usual may be afoot, or if it were that he has nothing to hide. He has planted stories in the political sketches, because what you hear three times is true; he has had the regular surveys shaped in various ways around the love and respect he enjoys among the mothers of this country, and the soldiers, and no doubt the tinkers, the tailors, the candlestick-makers—

The great question itself he has not yet put out, namely whether they want him at the head of a government. The government he currently serves is only halfway through its legal term but at the arse-end of its natural run—no government in this country has ever lasted much beyond its half-term, so it may be taken for granted that its natural run is precisely half the term stipulated by the dead letter of the law.

The supreme councillor is not going to commit himself, even before the perpetual closed-door session of his own mind's indulgent court, on whether he had any hand in arranging matters just so. His hands have always as it were benevolently hovered above the heads of the citizenry, in a gesture of mild benediction; how can they then be said to have meddled? In what way have they ever done anything that the body politic did not already tend to, of its own sweet will? He has never, as others have tried, grasped a blade and hacked about; he has never pushed and shoved. And if matters have always turned out just so, why, it is merely that he has anticipated the turn they would take, and seen that it was good.

It so happens that he believes this: that to govern successfully is not always to govern well, and indeed that to govern too well is sometimes to govern badly. One must always, he believes with the great political minds of antiquity, make more promises than one can keep, for otherwise the house would be empty of hopeful petitioners; one must, by the same token, leave a tolerable margin of discontent, not only to give the leader's hands always more work to do, but also to channel the discontent of the chronic malcontents, of whom there is never a dearth in any nation and who would else vent their frustration on truly valuable achievements or institutions and tear the place to pieces.

Be that as it may, the supreme councillor and the nation of which he is in a sense the guiding spirit have always found themselves unusually in tune with, and inseparable from, one another, their differences in temperament notwithstanding. Who is to say who guides whom, in the final analysis? They are many and one, in him.

The supreme councillor dropped off there for a minute, lulled by his soothing reflections. But the other one is still at it. He firms alliances and secures backing. He tots up votes, and compares best- and worst-case scenarios: if so much, then so much. He trades horses with the opposition, through a chain of intermediaries. A course of action takes shape, in the ministerial camp. Three strikes: first the daughter's wedding, then the unveiling of the initiative, to great public acclaim and universal media fanfare, and finally the vote of no confidence—

Doorstepped and harried increasingly by the press, now that the support figures are out and the government has reached its half-term, the minister is modest and loyal to the current leadership, and it is only perhaps in a certain stagey quality to his modesty that he betrays his ambition—why, this late in the day he seems to have adopted some of the Leader's mannerisms, a more restrained, more subdued, perhaps faintly ironic version of the famous baby-eyed, sphincter-mouthed simper.

Are you aware that many people in this country admire the firm leadership you have shown?—Simper.

Are you encouraged by the recent opinion polls?—Simper.

What is the next bold initiative we can expect from your ministry?—Simper; but yes, he hints, yes: there may be something in the pipeline that could make a decisive difference to a number of problems now plaguing society, though it is too early yet to unveil them—

Well, there you have it: always with the answers to the problems plaguing society. Always with the blanket solutions that leave no chink by which any light or air might get into the body politic, and no obscure playing fields left to the forces of chaos. Thus do all grand schemes come pregnant with their own destruction.

Still, if the circumstances were to require the supreme councillor to plumb for one or the other of these antagonists, it would be no contest; oh, no contest at all. What a pity, the supreme councillor sighs, that the minister does not like me. I stand, I suppose, for all that he despises, except what the Leader stands for; there is always so much to despise, for those of the reforming persuasion— I stand, I suppose, for the corrupt old order, entrenched privilege, tired entitlement, the grovelling and snivelling to no apparent purpose, and also, I suppose, for the recumbent tendency, the fat complacent ease on the vast wedding bed while the breeze gently stirs the gauze curtains and the natural forces go about their natural business of disintegration. And in this, thinks the supreme councillor, he is correct, except that I pivot and pirouette so nimbly, despite appearances, and except that such definitions are never more than half the story. And yet he wants me to preside at the daughter's wedding, that is the curious thing.

He is not so far above grovelling and tired entitlement, nor so fervently on the side of merit, hard work and progress, that he does not wish to bask a little in the reflection of my glory; he is essentially conservative in his instincts, that is another reason for the great fondness I have for him, unrequited though it may as yet be.

There is in truth no breeze to stir the gauze curtains: these are oppressive days, the sky heavy with static, and the pressure so low that you would faint were you ever to try and rise. And still the rain will not come, and the plants droop, and the plaintive cuckoo's call rings out in vain; perhaps elsewhere it comes down, briefly and bringing no respite, but not here, not in this stewing alluvial trough. The achievement, that is rarely mentioned, of building a capital city in this stewing trough! We make ourselves, reflects the supreme councillor, easy targets for scorn, we laugh at ourselves before anyone else, we moan and complain and act the fool, and stand on bare feet and bowed legs, head cocked to one side, and hop and sidle as circumstances require, but in the long run, well—

They are fussing again. A procession of aides insinuate themselves into the chamber, on their soft feet, with their flowery headnotes and their altogether pink and powdery air. And now the spokesman or elder, whose name escapes him, though he has been with him for many decades, makes to whisper again into the vast, pink, pendulous, generously furred ear.

'The time—' he says

I am, I assure you, the supreme councillor tells him, quite up-to-date on the developments.

'Of course.'

The aides, in their soft, windy, wafting way, hope to bring him news of the developments he has been so closely observing—though it might be argued that he has been observing them through his aides, so that were they to remain silent, perhaps the knowledge would never come to him, even as it seems that it came to him long before they spoke— Well, there is another question of a metaphysical nature that we shall not answer today.

—and I have been persuaded, by your soft persuasion, which as you know I hold in the highest regard, and which in some sense is merely an extension of my own persuasion, as it were redounding—

'Of course.'

You may in other words rest assured. What is required of me will be done, by me. I have never yet, as you well know, not risen to the occasion—

'Of course.'

—and shall not now fail to rise, if the circumstances—

'Your Excellency.'

Modesty requires that I should contradict you, but I shall not: it has perhaps been apparent to me since before you were born, though you too must by now be very old, and for all your soft footfalls somewhat creaky in the bones, and the knees prone to locking in the kneeling position, and the sphincter no longer—

'Your Excellency!'

Oh dear. Tell them at any rate yes. Tell them: yes, my excellency is willing to put in the required appearance, in consideration of the agreed consideration, on the appointed day, which remind me again—?

20

He rises, your Cabinet minister, from the marital bed, on the morning of his daughter's wedding. Eyes, slippers, bathroom, all much the same as every morning, except for the vibration in the veins, the powerline thrum. Things, he reflects as he pads down the stairs in his slippers, are essentially out of his hands; they will require now only the lightest of touches, a release of tension here, an increase of pressure there— His wife is not there to greet him when he walks into the kitchen: she has left with the daughter at the crack of dawn. They will be painted like pictures, and coiffed, and buffed, and primped, they and the bridesmaids and the handmaidens, and always a homosexual who has been appointed an honorary woman for the day, because he is so undeniably of the bride's side, not the groom's. The minister's breakfast cools on the kitchen counter. Yes, things are essentially out of his hands.

A maid goes about her business on soundless feet. The emptiness of the house exacerbates his nerves. Odd, that at this late stage in his career he should still suffer from nerves. He has faced down, he likes to think, criminals a great deal more dangerous than his present adversary, and faced them down with a slow reptilian pulse. He has carried out dawn raids with steady precision, he has addressed great crowds with equanimity. His daughter's wedding, on the other hand, and all that it entails make the nerves quiver like the string of the one-stringed fiddle. Well, so be it; the congee will do him good, with egg and sauce, and the coffee can hardly make it worse. And on to cigarette and shit, a calming ritual, though his stool is perhaps a little looser than usual, a little more urgent to emerge, and the sphincter more alive than usual to its passage.

He throws his cigarette into the bowl; it dies on top of his faeces with a satisfying hiss. Rinsed and patted dry he steps into the hall, where the maid looks at him expectantly.

'What?'

'The barber—' she says.

'Quite.' He forgot that he too would have to suffer an ordeal of primping.

She gestures in the direction of the terrace. Why do they keep him outside? The minister would not mind admitting the man into the house, where nothing is liable to cause him embarrassment, despite the soft, valanced aspect of the furniture his wife has chosen, nor anything so valuable as to justify fears of theft or pollution. Can his wife have given the order? Perhaps the maids, with their lively sense of hierarchy, made the decision in the spirit of their employers, as is so often the case in hierarchies, where the lowliest in rank are the keenest protectors of the status quo, much to the detriment of operations. Equally at the ministry, especially the border police.

How good it will be, to be shot of direct responsibility for the border police, its drab, recalcitrant mass, just a few days hence, and, come to think of it, of the police as a whole, with its Hydra-like vices. That alone will make the endeavour worthwhile.

—so that he almost bounds onto the terrace and startles the barber, who has been sitting on the bench dreaming into the garden. The barber jumps up and raises his hands, and the minister sketches his greeting—the swift, token greeting he is increasingly fond of, which says never mind all that, we are among ourselves here. The towel has already been draped over the back of a lounger, and as he takes his seat he reflects that the barber has to all intents and purposes become a friend, differences in rank and responsibility notwithstanding. They have talked so often about boxing over the years, desultorily, and in a general way about affairs of state —

The barber keeps his ear to the ground: he caters to gentlemen of all ages and classes, more or less, and every Tuesday he offers a special price in his shop to the boys from the local school, and no doubt rubs himself furtively against them, as was the habit of such professionals in the minister's youth. To this he has no objection; it is a mark of continuity.

Hairdressers have notoriously bad hair, and this barber too combs a few long sad dyed strands across his nut-brown pate, as if he never saw the inside of a barber's shop. It is a matter of regret to the barber, and a melancholy joke between them, that the minister refuses to have his hair dyed. No doubt the markup on the products is substantial. Today, lowering himself onto the footstool he carries with him, the barber begins with congratulations on the daughter's wedding, and asks who the *eminent person* may be who will preside at the wedding.

The minister is pleased that his system of leaks to the press appears to be working so well. The risk, in refusing to give a name, was that the press would simply make one up, so instead he leaked so many that the press decided, off its own bat, that the leaks were unreliable, and reported merely that *an eminent person* would be presiding. The phrase *an eminent person* has been much repeated and proved much better publicity than one or the other name could have done: on one of the television channels the minister's own mugshot was placed side-by-side on the infographic with a grey blob containing a question mark, the fourth or fifth item on the news.

'What have you heard?' he asks.

'They are saying the Leader —'

'No, not him. More —'

'More *eminent*?' The barber's neck bends reflexively before the notion.

'Well—'

'The supreme—'

The minister puts a finger to his lips, an uncharacteristic gesture he will need more time to practise. The barber's tired eyes widen and he makes a noise not unlike *oho*. The minister closes his eyes and leans back in the chair.

With clippers, scissors and comb, the barber goes to work. It has a soothing effect, to feel someone steadily at work on your head. Perhaps it stimulates the blood vessels, or evokes memories of our mother stroking our hair. The minister has no memories of his mother stroking his hair; they were not a physically demonstrative family, and communication was by and large barked. *Rare!* That was enough to convey a great many meanings, and to this day it gives him a homely feeling, to hear the sound ring out across the alleys of the old town, over the hardware's rattle and clank.

But when was the last time he heard it ring out? These days he sits in the official car, from one end of the city to the other, soundproofed, chilled to the bone—

'And I cannot persuade you—' the barber interrupts his reflections.

'Of what?'

'A little tint, a little natural—'

The minister is about to wave him off, but a thought stops him. Would it not be a fitting tribute to the daughter's wedding, as well as to the political battle ahead, to break with habit and have his hair dyed? There is an ancient tradition among warriors of going into battle looking their best.

'Will there be time?'

'It takes no time at all,' says the barber. 'This product—' which despite the years of disappointment he yet manages to magick out of thin air and hold up '—can be applied in no more than ten minutes.'

The minister looks at his watch. 'I suppose there is time—' he says uncertainly.

But the barber is already a-bustle, rummaging in his bag, waving excitedly at the maid, instructing her to bring a big bowl of water, and an extra towel, and some kitchen paper— No, thinks the minister, no man is a hero to his servant. There is no getting out of the dye-job now.

As the barber rinses his hair and applies the dye with a broad brush, the minister goes over the arrangements. Three strikes: first the supreme councillor's presence at the wedding, and with it a show of endorsement of the minister's ambitions, by the highest authority in the land. Next the announcement, come Monday, of his latest policy initiative. A masterstroke: it came to him unbidden one night, on the way home from one of the late meetings at their favourite restaurant, in the official car—

They had been driving down an empty road frozen in the vermilion of the sodium lamps, and the minister was staring with blank tired eyes out the window at the batteries of shuttered shophouse fronts, when all of a sudden he was jolted out of his daze by a roar of engines and blaring horns that rose up at them from behind, and gained on them, and washed over them in a flash of headlights, screams and shouts: some of the boys' voices had barely broken, he could tell in that flash, and the girls in flimsy clothes that clung to their backs were all puppy fat and hard shoes on large flat childish feet. They flashed by, a brief, violent disruption to the purr of the official car, and in that same flash it came to him.

A curfew.

To wit: no under-eighteens to be out alone after ten at night. No, make that nine. Fines, warnings, and the blame to be shared equally by the parents. Three months on a trial basis, and no reason why it should not be extended forever, if it sets minds at rest. He slapped his fist into the palm of his hand, there in the official car, with the icy air still a-tremble from the roaring flash of doctored scooters, to the bafflement of his driver. Order of the highest order. Joy among the mothers, who already love him. The popular press instantly on his side. A masterstroke.

That will be Strike Two.

And then, swift on its heels, the vote of no-confidence, tabled by the opposition. Already a faction within the party is said to be getting restive; the Snakes, as they are known to the press. That in itself will not be enough, but perhaps there will be one or two surprises on the day. Finance, like the minister himself, is not a member of parliament but commands a small group of forward-looking technocrats: they will blow where the wind blows, and by then it will blow his way. Sport, for all his inscrutable modern ways, is the offspring and avatar of a regional chieftain who has had one such avatar in every one of the last three governments. Culture and her dim-witted, reactionary clique. Health, crumbling under the Leader's impossible demands—

It will have to do. Last-minute horse-trading will swing it, but that too is essentially out of his hands.

'If your Excellency would care—'

It is difficult to say what the effect is. At first the minister recognizes nothing in the mirror, then the picture rearranges itself and he seems to see his younger self, perhaps from his heyday in the force, and then his face sets into waxen improbability under a tinted wig. Yes, a wig: that is the effect, not so much that the face is dead and the hair alive or vice versa, but that they occupy different planes, or different points in time.

'This will not do,' he tells the barber. 'I look—'

'Your excellency looks young,' the barber ventures, but there is no conviction in his voice.

The minister stares at the apparition. 'We will have to wash it out, will that do it?'

'It is not recommended, so soon after— There will be blotches.'

'Then what is to be done, man? This is a disaster.'

Again he must have spoken more forcefully than he would normally allow himself, because the barber's hands tremble and fuss ineffectually about the back of his head. 'Well?'

'There is— nothing to be done now,' says the barber, disconsolately. 'Perhaps if after another hour or two—'

'I do not have an hour, you absymal fool, this is the day of my daughter's wedding.'

The barber has shrivelled into himself, trying to occupy as little space as possible in the face of the minister's fury. The minister raises the mirror again and stares into his own waxen face, furiously.

'The eyebrows. You must do the eyebrows.'

The barber relaxes first fractionally, then substantially, then blossoms into joy. 'Of course,' he exclaims. 'What extraordinary— Yes, of course, I should have suggested it; that will make all the difference!'

The minister, fuming, forces himself to recline and shut his eyes while the barber bustles and fusses about the eyebrows, but he is zinging with anger still, and the waves must hit the poor idiot like static. A disaster, and this on a day when the massed press of the nation will descend on his daughter's wedding, and he must look his best for the cameras—

The farce could be spun out a great deal longer, thinks the supreme councillor, but his attention is irresistibly diverted by a smell of stagnant canal and damp wood, by a taste of metal on the tongue, a hollow sense of falling in the belly, the constriction of narrow walls and low overhangs along the walkways, and the sound of water slapping cement. Yes, she has reappeared: his favourite. It was time.

Is this the same hut? It is one very much like it, in the matter of floral PVC, of cigarette burns, of plastic bags on nails, to say nothing of the coconut fibre mattress: have we spoken of it before? It has seen a world of grief, the coconut fibre mattress, as far as couplings are concerned, and as far as lonely night sweats are concerned. Coconut fibre is a patient material, but its patience is not inexhaustible. Much like me in that regard, thinks the supreme councillor, and gives the mattress an affectionate pat, in his mind. Yes, he is inordinately pleased to see the old girl again. It is of course as a daughter that he is fond of her, not as a lover, as his favourite child in a nation who are all, in a manner of speaking, his children. Though my loins are rigorously, religiously barren, thinks the supreme councillor, I have a great many children to whom I am mother and father both, absent other mythical parentage.

Some races fancy themselves descended from giants or gods: fierce, warlike people who are often described as *proud* in inverse proportion to anything they might have to be proud

174

of. Not this one. We have all, thinks the supreme councillor, more or less sidled into our current place of abode, all the more securely and indisputably to make our home here. We are not fierce, nor are we warlike, nor do we present a greatly impressive spectacle on the international stage—unlike our current overlords, with their enormous armour-plated chests and their thick heads; and yet we endure, higgledy-piggledy, among the stagnant canals and the rotting wood and the two kinds of patterned PVC.

But the hair: was that not always a matter of concern for the woman? What happened to it? Now it takes rather the form of a mop or broom— And there is his answer, to the question where she might have been all this time: in prison, for her offenses, where they shaved her head, for largely hygienic reasons. Quite right too, thinks the supreme councillor, where would we be if everyone— And also he was correct in assuming that she was in a safe place whilst out of his sight. Now on the other hand: *in* his sight, and not so safe. What can that mean?

She is at her food again, her bowls of fish and rice and soup. That is encouraging. Back on track, you might say, and the old boil on her cheek still hard and red and obdurately in place.

The minister enters backstage into a world of flounces. There is a provisory aspect to the ballroom, as if this were not the angle from which the public would eventually see it and the room would subtly rotate just before they arrived, a few degrees to the north or south. The magnificence of ruched, bunched, massed and ruffled satin, or taffeta, or organdy, is evident even from here, in a preponderance of peach. But throughout there is disorder: of ballroom chairs still partly stacked, of bags and purses and half-drunk soft drinks, of the snaking lines and blocky shapes of electrical equipment, and even, here and there, an orphaned pair of shoes in a splayed or knock-kneed position. Waxed paper covers surfaces, fluorescent catches in crosshatched highlights. Flowers bristle. Staff mill. A disembodied voice, booming but muffled, counts out the numbers One, Two, Three, at random intervals.

At the most bunched and ruffled point, towards the far corner by the great panorama windows, a kind of circular stage or dais has been set up, garlanded, the minster thinks, to buggery. On it, a half-circle of chairs, all misproportioned gilt and chintz, and at the apex of the semi-circle, a throne. There is no other word for it: the vast oval of the back rest resembles a great heraldic shield or ballroom mirror, its face an expanse of shining purple; the seat would accommodate the most enormous arse. Well, the supreme councillor's arse is undeniably enormous, thinks the minister, it is just as well we made provision for it. Also a little bevelled, gilded and upholstered footstool, for the supreme councillor's enormous feet. Ancestral habit prompts the minister to wonder what the rental cost may be, by the hour, and how, in proposing the package, it would be itemised: *throne (optional)*—so much money.

His mood, sour still after the dyeing disaster, lifts a fraction. In the centre of the semi-circle, a low incidental table, flounced and valanced at the legs, lies as yet bare. It will in due course hold a representation of the dowry, in the shape of certain artful arrangements of what may look like, or indeed be, gold, and which in this country is due the parents of the bride. His mood lifts further. It has all already been accounted for and factored in: this, too, is the wife's department, and he has every faith that she has disposed wisely of whatever may be left once the cost of the young couple's house is taken off—

The minister himself affected reptilian abstraction during the barter between his wife and the groom's parents, who seemed to him an extraordinarily intent team, and extraordinarily voluble for such hardened businesspeople. They were like trawlers labouring in a choppy sea, the groom's parents, buffeted hither and yon by their commercial emotions. So long ago now —

The monks are to perform their business in the much smaller room next door, where a pediment has been set up for them with the paraphernalia. A the moment the room serves as a camp for the women; some have got here so early that their gala make-up is already in need of refreshing. Handbags litter surfaces. Two of them are already busy taking pictures. The minister shields his face, with its newly blackened eyebrows. A thick floral miasma hangs over everything, as if a hundred aerosols have been let off. His wife is busy with a floral shoulder piece and barely glances up.

'Oh,' she guffaws. 'You look —'

The bridesmaids giggle.

'Handsome,' pipes up one of them, the daughter's perennial best friend. Hard as nails, yet terrible luck with her men, that seems to be the general story. Perhaps there is such a thing as higher justice, no matter the chronology.

'Thank you,' says the minister. 'You are all beautiful, which given the investment in time and money is just as well.'

They make a sound not unlike *neee* high in their throats, and the wife gives a snort. It is not as though he is alone with the peculiar hair: the wife's stiff pompadour has ballooned to twice its size since he last saw her.

'If you are not busy, uncle —' she says.

'I am a busy man.'

'Yes. Tell the —' She flaps a be-ringed hand by her ear.

'Sound man,' one of the bridesmaids volunteers.

'Yes. Tell him to be done in ten minutes. This racket has

been going on—'

'*Rare,*' says the minister, not ungrateful for the excuse to leave them to it, and for the errand to take his mind off the coming ordeal.

It is in a way like coming home, this return to the quiet slum. The old stagnant smells are so familiar, the setup so reassuring. He has discovered the difference now: this hut has its own squat lavatory, in a little adjacent cell. My, thinks the supreme councillor, we have come up in the world. The bowl has been awkwardly cemented into a foundation that rises a good five inches above the PVC of the main room. You flush from a plastic bucket and shower from another. With the flexing and unflexing of her toes on the floor we are on firmer ground. Also the tingle between her shoulder blades, and the conversation—

It is time.

But for what? And how is one to quiet this racket without exerting a great deal of unnecessary force? Time for what? And what time is it? Early evening, as before. The morning of a new day. The distinctions, with old age, blur.

Yes, the conversation:

'—will you be ready?'

'Ready now. You come here?'

'In a while.'

'How long is a while?'

Ah, the old fighting spirit. It takes a tougher place than jail to beat it out of her, that too is reassuring to see. All stories in this country, reflects the supreme councillor, in a way go on forever; they have no beginning or middle or end, or rather they are all middle, with interruptions. Nothing ever ends here. Nothing dies, reflects the supreme councillor, but is absorbed back into the totality of all things and so goes on living; that is one way of looking at it.

Then why, at this late stage in his long life, is he so troubled? What is the weight that presses on his ancient golden heart and sends his pulse—well, not perhaps racing, but pulsing, as it has not pulsed for many a long year?

It is time.

Yes, but for what? My excellency hears you, but my excellency is evidently busy here, how hard can that be to understand?

She clicks off her phone and busies herself with the utensils. He wishes she would hurry up. *She* wishes she would hurry up, that is what he must be sensing, for the supreme councillor has all the time in the world— Today she pays no great reverence to the utensils or the substance; it is over in a flash, with a certain amount of spatter where the overheated substance jumps out of the tinfoil pan. She flicks the spatter off her shorts, balls the whole thing up and throws it into her own personal lavatory bowl. Two scoops from the bucket and the evidence, for what it is worth, is gone. They plumb well in the slum, thinks the supreme councillor, perhaps because they cannot afford to plumb badly. Though the grouting leaves something to be desired.

At least we have more or less got our bearings now; no time is entirely wasted, even here. With a little native wit—and it occurs to the supreme councillor that he has been coasting on his native wit all his life, the vast loads of learning notwithstanding—we can complete the picture to our satisfaction. On the telephone just now: the son. The matter in hand: a delivery. Ergo he has entered the business, as agreed after his foolish accident, and has been holding the fort while his mother was away. And now they work in tandem, that is pleasing to see, given the great importance this nation has always placed on filial ties, the very mortar and fabric—

It is time.

'Father.'

For a moment the minister is unable to place the appeal, which comes from somewhere behind his left ear, in which he has for some time suspected he may be going deaf. A petitioner? A pious underling? The term, in the language, admits of all these interpretations, in relation to the senior party. The more senior you get, the more you become in a manner of speaking *father* to all manner of unrelated folk. But no, he realizes as he turns in the vague direction of the appeal, the son has turned up.

'Yes?'

The son raises his hands in greeting. He looks well; in another context you might say he looks tanned. As a teenager the boy tended to a flabbiness that tapered at the ends, a girlish softness unaccompanied by grace. Now he has firmed up, and perhaps filled out in some places. Also the hair is cut more sharply— No, that is not it: he has had work done on his nose, that is what it is. Why was I not informed, wonders the minister, even as he recognizes that there would have been no benefit in informing him, for either of them. The wife will have paid for it. You forgot he was coming, he tells himself, your only son, whom you have never much liked.

Nor greatly disliked, for that matter; found uninteresting merely, compared to his sister, whose softness he shares but not her grace. But now there is perhaps a new confidence to the boy, thanks to the years of study abroad, the new nose, or the status conferred by his father's eminent position, who is to say? These things have a way of sorting themselves out by and by.

Inevitably, though, the son has brought another fellow, of about the same age or a little younger, with a darker complexion and a broader hand and foot, half a head shorter and in an overly tailored suit. This is no surprise to the minister, but he nonetheless gives the fellow his best reptilian stare.

The fellow's hands fly up and he greets the minister with the air of a startled rabbit. The minister allows himself to soften into a bare dip of the head and a lipless smile.

So much of my career, he reflects, first in the force and then as a minister of this government, has been spent startling people like rabbits. In the few months of patrol, which even those destined for officer positions were condemned to in his day, and are indeed condemned to still, he took some pleasure in the effect he had on miscreants taken *in flagrante delicto*: the sweating foreigner slinking out of the slum, the petty thief with his hoard of chipped hi-fi equipment. It was a forgivable indulgence, and he will be startling them for a while yet. Oh yes, in a little while he will be startling them as he has never startled them before.

For now, there are niceties to be observed. The flight, the weather, the studies. The son seems eager to relate his experiences, perhaps to distract from the dark-complexioned fellow. The minister inclines a kindly ear—the left, in which he may be going deaf.

'—kept us for two hours on the tarmac.'

The minister shakes his head, pats him on the arm, and makes a note to come down hard on the national carrier, ever a popular move. Perhaps a new chairman, to bring on side.

'You have seen your mother? She has tasked me—' He gestures in the direction of the sound man's trestle table.

'Yes,' the son says eagerly. 'She has already told us to keep an eye on the caterers, because she worries—'

Us, us: we must get the boy married, thinks the minister as he waves them off and makes his way over to the sound man; there is no reason why he should not marry now that his sister has. If a suitable woman can be found, they can come to their own sleeping arrangements by and by, within reason. A decent fitting-in, that is the aim of the institution, all else is arrant sentimentality. It is precisely the Leader's failure to keep his feckless son from making an idiot of himself that suggests a crack down the man's entire moral spine. Put your own house in order, else there will always remain, in the public mind, the sense that lies are being told too blatantly on television, and the naysayers and malcontents will swarm like flies to the crack, which soon begins to suppurate with the infections they plant. Eggs, is it? The minister has no further interest in the metaphor.

21.

One by one the guests arrive, or else in twos and threes. Also aides. The police detail is being reinforced with each arrival entitled to such protection. The minister made it clear in advance that sirens would not be welcome, though one or two can be heard blaring, briefly, outside. These could of course be passing along the road about other business, but the minister, at the edge of his preoccupied mind, suspects that one or two of the guests cannot resist it, or have forgotten the simple courtesy that was asked of them, to say nothing of the vast potential for error inherent in the simplest manoeuvre.

Looking down from the ballroom windows he has a general sense of gleaming blackened glass and intent chaos, with the stiff starched silks in all the colours of the rainbow or the white-and-gold fantasy uniforms of the patriotic element, picked out like boiled sweets on a granite countertop. Of the supreme councillor as yet no sign. Twice, between other duties, he has phoned the supreme councillor's people, and twice a recorded message has informed him that the number cannot be reached. An aide or two are busy clarifying the situation—it would be like the Leader's communication networks to give out at a time like this.

And yet he has confidence, perhaps for the first time today, and allows himself for the first time to feel the festive atmosphere, the elation of impending joy. Two solid families, and two solid young people, are being joined after all, in circumstances of extraordinary prosperity and privilege. Extraordinary: it is not the police detail, nor the money lavished on the celebrations, but the size, in relative terms, of the influence concentrated here. Every other guest could rally a small town to his or her service, or a biggish one, depending, including the commercial and religious establishment and the intricate mechanisms of the Town Hall. And then there is the ludicrous aspect, of the dyed hair and the starched silks, in all the colours of the rainbow, the festive folly —

The minister himself is dressed in a plain black suit, a golden necktie his only extravagance. Well, that and the dye job. The wife picked it out for him, the tie, but moving among the company and feeling eyes occasionally arrested by it, he thinks of it now as a suitable homage to the guest of honour and presiding spirit. Its ironic tint is visible only to himself. For it is sometimes said, in private, that the supreme councillor is turning into a golden effigy of himself, and that it would not be very strange to find the entrance to his famously modest residence flanked by a pair of two such as himself, fixing the visitor with their benevolent gaze, and a third in the inner sanctum, and that you might come away without ever figuring out which had been the real one.

Today that is all that is required, thinks the minister as he raises and drops his hands and ducks his neck in perpetually modest greeting of friends and acquaintances: whether the supreme councillor wishes to maintain a mysterious silence or utter ineffable banalities, it is all for the good.

Here is Sports, in a white-and-gold fantasy uniform that he somehow manages to wear with an air of detachment, as if it had happened to walk in beside him without his encouragement. They greet each other as affectionately as two reserved men of different ages may. Sports murmurs his congratulations, and the minister asks when it may be time for Sports to take the same important step. Sports smiles blandly.

'I had my eye,' he says, 'on your Excellency's daughter, but I suppose —'

'Well,' says the minister, 'that is unfortunate. I wish I had another, in light of the connection that would afford me with one of the most—*influential* families of the—'

Sports nods a sportsman's respect at the allusion to his father, a celebrated fugitive from justice and headman of a large swathe of the western coast—as well he might, since the minister has so far forsaken his duty to apprehend the man who, as everyone knows, lives in comfortable retirement on the family estate.

'Hope springs—' says Sports.

'Indeed,' says the minister, patting his arm. 'And your Excellency is young.'

'Talking of hope,' says Sports, 'I hear there are developments afoot to which this occasion—'

The minister puts a finger to his lips, more confident already in the gesture. 'We will speak further,' he says, 'but I see Culture has steamed into port; if your Excellency will excuse me—'

'Your Excellency.'

In the purview of the ludicrous long lenses of the press, the minister greets Culture and her retinue. He is humble, dry, reasonable, yet he always feels that Culture has a kind of reverence for him that seems surprising from a woman so wholly defined by her snobbery. Perhaps she is shy under the bovine exterior, and grateful for the even, humble dryness with which he treats her: that he does not thrust himself on her notice as more forceful colleagues will. She nods a slightly pursed appreciation of the arrangements; it is important to her that things should be done correctly. Hence her post, which is perpetually held by women just like her, who are only required once or twice a year to address the public, usually after the great boisterous holidays, on what is and is not compatible with the country's culture, and otherwise to stall any projects that might bring the nation to the notice of the international cultural establishment, so called. They are invariably wrong in these pronouncements, because of course the culture is whatever it is, including the boisterousness of its holidays, but that is beside the point. Yes, he must keep her in the job, she is made for it.

These thoughts carry him through a meandering account of some inconvenience that befell her and her retinue on the way to the event.

'Well,' he says, 'your Excellency has come, that is what matters. We should have been very sorry to have missed you.'

'Your Excellency is very kind,' she says. 'I would not have missed it for the world. And is it true—'

'Not at all,' he says, with a smile that could go either way.

She interprets it her way and tilts in a little, as a large makeshift structure may list after long rains, or a moored yawl. 'And it is all,' she says, 'very *timely*.'

'Ah, time—' the minister quotes himself. He can count on the fingers of one hand the conversations in the last two decades or so that held his interest. So she is on side, as he knew she would be. Over the heads of the crowd, or through them, he catches the wife's eye and slightly shakes his head at her. No answer as yet from the supreme councillor's people, or for that matter the supreme councillor.

'If your Excellency would—' he says.

'Of course,' says Culture, satisfied with her allotted time.

But at that moment the phone rings again. When the woman answers hello? hello? there is nothing but indistinct voices and the sound of motors. Someone is barking assertively; someone else is grumbling, and a motorcycle revs as if underfoot.

'Hello?'

There is nothing but this for several more seconds; the phone must have gone off in the son's pocket, so she hangs up.

Oh, thinks the supreme councillor, but is that the only possible conclusion, my dear good harried woman? Listen now, listen: what is it these voices are saying? Who are they talking to if they are not talking to you?

The supreme councillor's enormous stomach tightens. Terrible wind, ill wind. No, he is not as young as he was. Indigestion is new to him, an affliction of middle age that never afflicted him in middle age and is out of proportion, surely, to the shenanigans in hand, which are wholly familiar and by and large maintain a kind of natural justice among these striving forces.

Calm now, calm, he tells himself. Through me these striving forces flow; through me they are in equilibrium.

Not now!

To let them flow, unobstructed, like wind and water. Calm now. All is as it must be and were it otherwise would not be as it is.

The phone rings again. She raises it to her ear and, though the supreme councillor wills her to listen closely this time, clicks off with an irritable frown. Well, we have no agency in the detail, that has always been a slight regret. We may marshal vast forces, but the small ones, well—

Again the phone rings, and this time she clicks it off without looking. The irritation only spurs her to greater hurry down the swaying walkways and bouncing planks. Wrong, all wrong; foolish impatience: how often has he pointed it out, in his increasingly gnomic speeches to the masses? It became a winged word, at the height of his powers, among the masses. *We must be patient.* Even the knockabout comedians used it to some effect, at one time. *We must be patient*, they squawked with a mock-solemn air, yet they understood the truth of it perfectly well and helped, in their way, to hammer it home. But at the microscopic level—

Calm now. Let the still centre hold, and spread even into the farthest reaches of the land. Let it hold and spread and envelop every man and, more to the point, woman, and—why not?—child in the land. Let it spread and enfold them and keep them safe. Let it—

I said not now.

'Ah yes,' smiles the Leader as the hooded baby eyes take in the room. 'All very— And of course the arrangements in every way the way you want arrangements like that, and you know'—this confidence to no one in particular—'when a thing like that happens it is in a way better if the arrangements are all what you call *the highest order*—' Here the head dips and the sphincter mouth forms a little moue of modest appreciation, or amusement, who is to say?

'Your Excellency is very kind,' the minister says as drily as he knows how, though inwardly he is getting worried by the radio silence from the supreme councillor's people. Flashlights strobe around them, making him avert his eyes. The Leader basks.

'No, because you know when the arrangements are like this and there is like you say'—the minister is unaware of having said anything—'some kind of give and take, you know, but of *the highest order*, then— And it is nice for the guests also when they come and they do not know, you know, what will come and who will come and when what will come, that is like— *television.'*

The Leader looks inordinately pleased with the analogy, and glances at his wife, whose mouth twitches at his wit. A cat-like woman, the minister confirms to himself, so sleek and plump and all but purring at the snug fit of her designer outfit. And her hands too are a little like a cat's paws: soft and plump and squeezable they look, and if you pressed the tip of your finger into the soft dry centre of her palm, out would come the dainty little claws and close around it, and nick it perhaps in the area of the nail bed— Were the minister any younger he would have said he fancied her, all the more because she so clearly despises him, so that a degree of scuffling would be inevitable, followed perhaps by a longish sulk on the windowsill, or under the armchair. Then you would give her her milk.

'—with that temple also we had a very good experience,' the Leader is saying, 'and of course then it cost a lot more money than we thought when they came in that time, you remember?' This to the wife, who smiles enigmatically. 'And we had, what, ninety-nine for luck and health and prosperity because that was what they said is the best number, I do not know how many you have here but I think maybe not ninety-nine for luck and success, and there was a price but I do not remember what it was, only that it was a lot more than we thought when we estimated the offering that would—'

Whatever stratagem occupies the Leader's wife's mind as her husband drivels on seems to put her in a benevolent mood, because she fairly nods at the minister when he murmurs his dry assent, as if at least on the level of the enormous cost of such undertakings they could be assumed to have some understanding.

Superstitious as all-get-out, the Leader: has an astrologer set the date for all his best business decisions, private or public, the distinction is meaningless. Perhaps that is what she is nodding at the minister for, the recognition that they are both married to highly superstitious people. But his thoughts are drifting; he tells himself to focus on the business in hand.

'—so people say what and we have to reform them in some way, and I think that is good if we reform them so that anyone, or even women, can come and do that, and then we have the support of some reforming groups also, but also it is a difficult thing because as you say'—the minister has said nothing—'you do not want to upset the—'

'—apple cart—' says the minister.

'—because then they think you want to upset all the institutions or, you know, communism'—the wife's mouth purses in pretty disgust—'and then when one country falls then the next one will follow and then before you know it—'

With the Leader's thought processes thus in freefall, the minister looks around for an aide's eye to catch. The Leader's wife notices and puts a plump hand on the Leader's arm.

'But we must let his Excellency attend to his—*arrangements*,' she says.

The Leader stops in mid-sentence, frowns, then ducks his head twice and purses his mouth in eager assent. 'Of course,' he says.

'Your Excellencies,' says the minister, and with a bow to both makes his way over to the private room. Behind him, he thinks he can hear the words *the highest order*, spoken in an indefinable tone.

They form a huddle, his aides, and his wife is there, furious.

'What is this?' she hisses.

'It seems the signal—' the minister says lamely.

'The signal? No one else, no one, has trouble with the *signal* here.'

The minister turns on his aides.

'Has everything—has *anything* been done to find him?'

These are his closest and most trusted aides, and there is an air of hurt about them when they explain that yes, anything and everything has been done. Phone calls are being made at five-minute intervals to all known numbers of all the supreme councillor's perfumed people, and not one can be reached *at this time*—the recorded message having for a while now taken on a portentous ring. At this time of all times. Even now one of the aides bends to his phone to try again. For a moment they all stare at the man, then he drops it and looks anywhere but into their faces. The last of the supreme councillor's people to answer, forty-five minutes ago, murmured something soft and reassuring before apparently turning off his phone. Since then, nothing.

'And other—?'

Yes, so too any sympathetic associates and former associates of the supreme councillor's who could at all be tracked down, in senior Army posts or comfortable retirement—at death's door in hospital, one. They pledged to do their best, or exhorted them to be patient, or have faith, and more such phrases. The closest they came was with the deputy chief of the Army, who is tentatively on side and here today, and who immediately sequestered himself in a private room to work what magic he could, and emerged a quarter of an hour ago, shrugging. Not one but two couriers have been dispatched to the supreme councillor's residence, young officers who volunteered to ride pillion on police motorcycles, weaving through the traffic as fast as they could and deploying the siren where necessary.

One of them is standing outside the gate even now and has reported no sign of life—no maids in the gardens, no security, no fans stirring in any outbuildings where that could be spotted from the road, no air conditioner compressors at work, not even a dog barking. Just the great flame tree shimmering in the sun and the bamboo looking parched, and the long garden wall all lichen and flaking paint. The great iron knocker on the gate sounded small and dull when he hammered on it, and when he pressed the bell there was no telling whether it was even wired up. Once, the putter of an engine approached down the narrow road, and the officer squared his shoulders, but when it came it was a motorcycle taxi, and the driver went past without giving them a second look.

'Nonsense,' barks the minister. 'There is a permanent police post at the mouth of the street, manned by never fewer than two men in rotating shifts. The state pays for it; I see the bills. I *approve* the bills, as if I had nothing better to do, under special dispensation—'

The aides look shamefaced.

'What?'

'It seems that too is empty.'

'And the local station?'

'They say they understand that the—is not at home.'

'—which could of course,' ventures one aide, 'mean that he is on his way—'

The minister looks at him hard while the others shrug or search the carpet for clues. Blue, the carpet, with flecks of carrot and mustard woven in, like vomit. *The highest order*.

Presently the double doors swing slackly open and there stands his daughter, in her own great shining halo of white, ready for the wedding. The heart lurches, and the minister feels a blush rising all the way to his newly-dyed hairline. He

192

has not blushed since adolescence, and was even then rarely given to blushing. His daughter's hair glistens with the gloss of youth, and she looks as if she is radiating light from within, with the joy of the day or the pearly makeup. To have let his daughter down. He exchanges a glance with his wife, out of the corner of his eye, and in the instant it is clear that he will have to break the news to the girl.

Spreading his arms, lowering his head, he takes a breath and walks over to the girl, and has no sooner reached her than her face seems to swell and bloat and tears rise in her eyes like a flood.

Along the canal she strides, on the raw concrete walkway, with great vigorous strides. She marches, yes, a soldier in her cause: let it never be said that the dear woman is anything but vigorous in the execution of her various tasks, from keeping the hut spick and span to the errands that are thrust upon her, or chosen, either which. The water, slopping an ill jade green and quite dull on top, with a covering of dust or dead insects that never seems to subside into the depths, smells of rot. How calmly it slops. Halt a little, the supreme councillor urges her, and contemplate these waters; is it not truly said that in the contemplation of water may be learnt a great many lessons? For example, here, how to stagnate when there is wisdom in stagnation, and nothing at all to be gained from marching, soldier-fashion—

No, on she strides. No agency. Well.

—and gains the street, an ill-defined cul-de-sac where weeds proliferate on one side and flooding never fully subsides for weeks on end, and where on a bench hewn together from old scaffolding wood should be sitting at all times, or at least lying, a boy, one of several in rotating shifts. There is no one now. He must have gone to piss or get a drink. A scooter stands there, and a shirt hangs from a nail. He will be back.

But when?

The phone. Click. On. She will give him an earful in a minute or two, by the twenty-four-hour convenience store, to harry her so. Lights are already coming on in the fat, sullen late afternoon. On.

Momentum, reflects the supreme councillor, takes on its own momentum at a certain point, and perhaps there is now nothing he or she can do to stop her, and the fact of the encounter is already fully pre-formed—unless perhaps some superior momentum, such as an out-of-control lorry, were to intervene, radically and at such cost to those involved that the intervention could never be justified. You picture shattered glass, twisted steel, small dice. Or perhaps there is a greater force still at work that ensures the even distribution—

Procrastination has always stood him in good stead when inaction alone would not do.

Not so today. From this calm vantage, here on the great wedding bed, he can see a thousand little signs that might stop her: the fellow in the suit, suddenly turning to retrace his steps. The parked van. The stillness of the two cashiers in the twenty-four-hour convenience store, in the blinding white-and-green light. The son's pleading eyes, come to that, if only from this distance she could see them. Ah, but she is getting a little short-sighted in her middle age, and vanity prevents her from admitting it, and at any rate the execution of tasks like this requires a certain narrowing of the visual field, a steeling of the mind against the lurching signal from the innards—

So she approaches, briskly, and is about to launch into her tirade, with a half-comical raising of the arms, and words form, regarding his incontinent way with the telephone, and come to think of it his general incontinence and uselessness, and though he moves a hand furtively and his eyes plead, she is too far gone now to notice.

They step out fast, from behind the parked van and the corner of the convenience store, where there is a set-back gravelled lot large enough to conceal the motorcycle with two uniformed officers, in addition to the plainclothesmen. They dart or rev, depending, and have encircled them before she even shuts up.

Shouts. The usual.

The last task falls to the rookie on the back of the bike, who assumes the stance like a puppet; it has not yet become second nature. Left leg, right leg, in his awkward boots. Shoulders squared. And then he fumbles with all the kit on his belt to get the handcuffs out, and in the sudden silence brought about by this delay, something passes between the plainclothesmen.

Mother and son are kneeling on the ground, already half-resigned. But now, unaccountably, the grip on their twisted arms eases, and the shiny boots step backwards, calmly, deliberately, and out of the corner of her eye she sees the opening, and runs for it.

22.

But what a beautiful day it turned out yet, a feast in the end for all the senses. The catering too was of *the highest order*. And the bride so beautiful, her eyes shining with freshly dried tears; the groom so handsome, if somewhat thin on top, and large of foot, and taut around the middle in his starched silks.

For music that afternoon they had a string quartet in evening dress, because the wife had so admired the gimmick, during their stay in the Old World, in an upmarket shopping arcade. It had proved easier to book than you might think and was exquisite torture to the minister's unmusical ear. A fresh-faced white man with eager glittering eyes sawed away at the first fiddle, and the cello swung passionately hither and yon, between a pair of Greek sandals with terrifying heels. Culture remarked on it, as did one or two of the society figures the wife and daughter have been cultivating.

An ironic lady with cropped hair who was dressed in a sort of high-grade sack, to all intents and purposes happily married to someone with a name that goes on for too long, remarked how refreshing it was to be spared the interminable noodling of the so-called traditional music, on the bobbin-operated zither. It was unclear which part her irony was meant to be most dismissive of, the problem or the solution.

The minister startled himself with the virulence of his contempt for the woman. How hard he found it to stifle, on this pivotal day in his life, with so many other things to occupy his mind. It came over him like a lorry-load of sharp stones, this loathing, and perhaps the poor woman had only meant to be friendly the only way she knew how. From a very old family, you could tell from the way she disdained the pompadour of the aspiring classes, and the starch of their silks. These people, thought the minister, no matter how they are fast-tracked in their globetrotting, and no matter how confidently they handle the fish knives or foie gras on the international stage: their allegiance to the supreme councillor and all he stands for is total. And of course she recoiled, despite the minister's best effort to stifle his contempt and despite the bland face he turned on her, and the bland unfinished phrase, and left him alone, and was lost to him as an ally—she and the husband with the over-articulated name, and no doubt their brood if they had any, all lost to him now—

But if he was not at his best, with so many things to occupy his mind, then everyone else around him made up for it twice over. They shone. It struck the minister later, as he leafed through the unimaginable number of photographs, official and unofficial, that had been taken by unimaginable numbers of photographers, most of whom he had never noticed: how people shone, in the greater concentration of the hotel's ballroom suite; no longer looking like boiled sweets but rather like so many plump precious jewels, in their starched shining silks and their glossy black hair; and even the minister himself, despite the many things then on his mind, gave in the pictures the impression of being fully one of their number, in his good black suit and the golden necktie, which although it had now lost its ironic point nonetheless gave the impression, as did everything else in the pictures, of extraordinary prosperity and complacency, of lives well lived to people's own satisfaction, and of a calm power in which to rest.

Yes, even the hair, which had so agitated him in the morning, looked in the pictures like exactly the sort of hair one ought to be sporting on such a festive occasion.

Here is the minister surrounded by his family: the wife in the double-sized pompadour, gleaming; the son, with his new-found air of ease; the minister's sister, not at all out of place

197

here in her Sunday best, which is rather better than he imagined it, given the time she spends barking at the old overland lorries. His sister is wearing a smile quite free of vinegar or salt, and her cheeks have filled out, so that an uninformed onlooker might be hard-pressed to put her on the bride's or groom's side. Has she found happiness late in life with a companion, perhaps a widowed school friend, or thanks to some other fortuitous development? He was too preoccupied at the time to tease it out of her, but must soon.

Here is the minister with Cabinet colleagues: Culture, Sports, and yes, even the great silky form of Foreign Affairs, who materialised in the room as soon as the coast was as it were clear, with his dainty little wife in the pointed shoes. Both are smiling benignly and the minister, search his heart as he might, can find in it no case against the sleek old chancer.

Here, too, is the minister with other high-ranking officials, including the permanent first secretary for education, now under investigation for being unusually rich after a burglary at his home revealed a stash of millions that could not be accounted for by his official earnings; and the deputy chief of the Army, who kindly found time to drop by. The only absence is the minister's best friend, superintendent of the capital's most lucrative police station, who had days in advance given notice that his mother was gravely ill and not likely to live the week. He was missed, but not grievously, given the general calibre of the guests and the incessant string of pleasantries that kept the minister on his toes.

Here are the young people: the bridesmaids foremost, in peach or salmon silk dresses that look tensile enough to stand on their own feet; the son again, and his young companion, who proved a great success with the women, thanks to his nimble conduct on the dance floor, at a later stage. Here are other members of the young couple's circle, the men on the whole fleshy before their time, the women of a pearly quality that has but recently become apparent to the minister among the young. They are pearly all over, from teeth to skin to shoes, and where legs and ankles are revealed those are pearly too. We were not, reflected the minister at the edge of his preoccupied mind, so pearly in our day, nor met anyone so pearly, nor saw anyone so pearly even in the pages of the colour magazines. Human history, he reflected at the time, is properly understood perhaps as a great progress towards ever greater pearliness, among the pearly classes.

There it was again, the inappropriate levity: he had in the end fortified himself with a couple of whiskies and experienced the rest of the festivities in a pleasant glow that was wholly appropriate, and yet wholly inappropriate, to the proceedings.

And here is the Leader, beaming, wormy mouth stretched in an ineradicable smile of triumph, yet with a becoming touch of modesty to the carriage of the square head and a coy cast of the hooded eyes. He looks, the Leader, to all intents and purposes like the Empress Whatshername, perched on the expensive hired throne, framed above the waist by the ornate oval gilt frame of its backrest, and the knees bent daintily to one side as if frozen in a curtsey, instead of, as the supreme councillor would no doubt have placed them, lazily apart to reveal a floppy bulge between enormous thighs. White fantasy uniform with gold epaulettes, and on his chest a collage of the Order of the Boot, the Order of the Bribe, the Eminent Fellowship of This-That-and-the-Other, such as accrue to public officials and captains of industry in the course of their career, and on his feet a pair of patent-leather shoes—can they be a figment of the minister's imagination? They are cut off in the photographs.

There at any rate he sat, the Leader, presiding over the proceedings with benevolence and modesty and a general air of somewhat saccharine, somewhat prissy *leadership*, with

---

199

occasional sly glances at the wife, who at one point sneaked up and placed a calming cat's paw on his shoulder, lest perhaps he enjoy himself too much in his triumph and get out of hand.

And talking of hands, the minister noticed that he had never noticed them before, the Leader's hands: they were unusually white and featureless, devoid of character except in the matter of their whiteness, which had perhaps a slightly yellow tinge; quite long, quite thin, but not the hands of an artist or musician, in the traditional associations of refinement, nor tapered and ineffectual, but merely another ill-fitting component in the overall ill-assembled whole that is the Leader's earthly carcass—head, face, eyes, mouth, long torso, low-slung-arse—but that no longer gives any hint of the ungainliness he must have had as a boy, and has rather come, thanks to the normative power of wealth and influence, into its own as just another undeniable possibility—odder perhaps than most when considered in its particulars, but in its overall effect not nearly as startling as it should be.

These were the hands, then, that symbolically joined those of the minister's daughter and her groom in matrimony, using the traditional length of blessed string tied loosely twice and three times. The couple knelt modestly on the dais either side of the Leader's patent-leather shoes, which he raised prissily on tiptoe during the ritual, perhaps to keep them clean of stain, or from some other unconscious impulse in his musculature that comes into play whenever he engages in one of the higher offices, where he must surely even now experience a residual sense of imposture. How much more briskly and effortlessly the supreme councillor, the treacherous swine, would have handled the task, with what superior casual dignity, and good humour, and sheer easeful, playful authority—

200

—and runs, not towards the unknown crowds and cover of cars that lie just a few hundred metres to one side, but like a hunted animal home to her lair, to the false sense of safety with which it glows in her muddled, frightened, unthinking mind.

They give her a good head, the boots, they take their sweet time about the pursuit, but once they get going they pound the pavement, as institutional boots have since time immemorial pounded the pavements, in hot pursuit. Sharp high flat barks, the ugly fury of little men, which is directed at nothing, and the more furious for it, and must be exercised off the leash every now and again.

Along the road she runs, and into the driveway of a public building, and left along its utilities and rubbish dumps, which at least provide an occasional break in the line of sight and a kind of cover, from boots and barks in hot pursuit. Oh, they have smelt it now and their lungs expand, and their hearts pound with the furious joy of the hunt. They all know where she is going, the woman, the men, it is in a way—thinks the supreme councillor—like the dog races, there is only one way they will ever go, round and round the track. Here is a porter of some description, pushing a tall steel cage of dirty washing before him and calling to a friend before he comes to a halt: if she were to throw herself on the ground here, by the porter's feet, and scream at the top of her lungs, perhaps the aborted sport and presence of witnesses would yet earn her no more than a hard kicking and a few months in jail—

But she is past already, these thoughts are no sooner thought than they are idle. And what time, when all is said and done, is it? Is what is happening now happening *now*, in view of the narrative tense? Has it already happened, in view of the microscopic lapse of time between observation and consciousness? Is it a foregone conclusion, and might thus happen any time in the future and be no different for it? Is this the time for such reflections?

He seems on second thoughts to have all the time in the world, as the feet no longer pound pavement but soggy dirt and old rotten boards, going thumpety-thumpety along the narrow walkways, stumbling here and there and scraping a shoulder or elbow against the wooden walls. The back way? Who knew there was a back way, and why does she not always take it, across the piece of waste ground at the back of the utilities? Well, they have their superstitions, and their habits—

There is time for insight in the hottest pursuit, and slack in the tightest action. The woman hits the wall of her hut with the flat of her hand, like a child playing tag, and stands for a moment stupidly blinking, as if the game must now stop; but it does not stop, the boots are upon her, a pack of men panting with hard directed fury, and their dull little guns out, firing flat thin cracks with a flat thin echo among the huts—*pekka, pekka*—and it dawns on her at last that this is the last place she wants to be—

At this last the supreme councillor is unsure what he is feeling. Horror or boredom, or a mixture of both, or merely the truth, long forgotten, of horror: that it is always, essentially, boring, and always, essentially, the same.

23.

The phrase *every square inch of the country* keeps ringing in the minister's head, on his ringing march along the ministerial corridor. Well, the Leader lost no time. The blood still rises into the minister's face, this Monday morning, at the memory of their conclave. But if the humiliation is to be recalled, then it should also be remembered that the conclave, in the small private room with the handbags and makeup cases and discarded shoes, was mercifully brief. Few words were needed between them, and they did not once catch each other's eye. The Leader had banked like a good speculator on this turn of events, and now that events had turned his way he wasted no time.

These were the considerations: that the minister, finding himself short of one *eminent person* to preside at his daughter's wedding, was in need of another; that the proposed replacement was in no way inferior to the person originally envisaged, and was indeed in some particulars superior; that this point needed to be given due and proper expression in a few dry, well-chosen phrases, here in the detritus-strewn room, to assuage any doubts either party might still entertain about it; and that, given the evident advantage that fate had as it were thrown into the minister's lap, a certain price had to be paid, of which the less said the better.

All this passed between them, a full understanding; the words they spoke were few and it was over sooner than perhaps either of them had expected. There remained only the formality of acknowledging that such an event, being very public in nature, created to the public eye a fresh and as yet nebulous web of familial obligations for both parties, in which both, considering the immediate overall advantages, were content to allow themselves to become enmeshed, as it were on a speculative basis—

There followed a silence when the minister's eyes momentarily lost focus, and he nodded slowly a few times into the middle distance, perhaps thirty degrees to the Leader's left. It struck him that he had not slept enough these past few months of plotting and scheming, and that he would very much like to sleep now.

'Right,' said the Leader at last, a short thin bark of resurgent impatience.

The minister pulled himself together. 'Right,' he said. And they put on their public faces, and walked almost companionably into the ballroom.

Yes, the blood still rises, but then it passes, and the phrase *every square inch of the country* asserts itself again. It was on the news last night—trust the Leader not to rest on a Sunday— and on the news again this morning; it is all they can talk about on the news, the new initiative, the new committee at whose head the Leader has placed himself. Every square inch of the country. Oh, it was a masterful move; he has until this day failed to take full account of the Leader's political acumen, or of the Leader's wife's. Never before in his long experience, first behind the grimy desks of the force, then in the musty corridors of power, has the minister seen any other man so completely outmanoeuvred, nor a man so careful of each step so completely hoist with his own petard. They have wrested the sword of righteousness from me and skewered me with it like a pig, he thinks, placing the business end in a fork as it emerges from my arse, to roast me all round.

Trounced. But though he may be finished he is perhaps not done. His steps ring out still, on the terrazzo. There are men under his care, flapping despite appearances like beached mackerel; he can fairly hear the wet flutter of their tails all the way down the tall mouldy corridors outside his office. He has a last responsibility to them. If his range of operation has shrunk to barely more than nothing, he hopes very much to occupy it to the utmost of its capacity to the last. Though he is very tired, he may perhaps strain a little against the shackles, let no one say that he went completely without a fight.

Before him, in the eternal shaded gloom, sits his best and oldest friend, for want of another. Once the entourage is gone the two men speak in a low murmur. A note has passed hands, a few scribbled words, whose tiny shreds are even now smouldering in the ministerial ashtray. In his mind they have combined with the news in the papers; the combination terrifies him.

After so many years the minister can see that his friend is agitated, placidly though he sits in the ministerial sofa. He is even, perhaps, acting in haste by coming here, the Monday after his mother's death. In the final analysis, the minister thinks, sitting opposite the superintendent of police, I have only himself to blame. I knew I would outlive my usefulness, but I had hoped perhaps for greater usefulness than I was granted. Despite my many years in the force and the corridors of power, I did not fully grasp the Leader's enormity; or rather I did, but I talked myself out of it. Here is a man, the minister remembers thinking the first time he met the Leader, who is morally null, and who will stop at nothing. And then he remembers thinking, when the offer of high office came, that no one can be wholly null, and no one stops at nothing at all. He counted on the Leader's cowardice if nothing else. He counted on his own wit. No, he has no one else to blame.

'You will of course follow these orders,' he tells his friend.

'The numbers—' says the superintendent, opening his eyes wide.

The numbers, multiplied by the police stations in the country, are by the minister's rough calculations staggering. In all the long years of the insurgency, not one-third as many were killed.

'Even so.'

There are, he thinks, good officers who will drag their feet, and accept the transfer to some godforsaken backwater or inactive post with which they have been threatened, should they fail to produce the stipulated number of corpses. There are orchards and small lumber businesses waiting for them, or scaffolding operations. Car parts. Let us hope their children are grown. But this air of corruption that hangs about the superintendent, the sense of shifting depths that has prevented him from rising in the official hierarchy, also means that he cannot be expected to be a hero now. The minister does not blame him. For all his powerful personality, it is comfort the superintendent craves. That is how he is made. Large forces are at his disposal, but they are chosen to ensure the greatest possible comfort, material or otherwise, for the superintendent. If the superintendent has lives on his conscience, as the minister is sure he does, then they were merely collateral: they got in the way of his ease.

The mechanics are now quite clear to him, in their fox-trap precision. Suppose you issue a quota: so many drug peddlers to be taken alive or dead, with the aim of cleansing *every square inch of the country* of their evil presence. And who can doubt that it is evil? And what has due process ever achieved against them? Suppose further that you suggest the compilation of a blacklist, at each police station across the country, of the *known offenders*. The worst of the worst. Suppose you set an ultimatum: the quota to be achieved, say, three months from now, or face transfer or demotion.

And suppose you then permit yourself to be overheard, by a trusted aide, as specifying that by alive or dead you mean both: so many alive, and so many dead.

That is what his friend's scribbled note said. He has no reason to doubt it; he could see it in the faces of the officers milling about in the corridors. These are terrified men, which is why their tails are flapping. That many of them would as soon kill you as look at you is neither here nor there: it is the straight floodlit vista that frightens them, the systematic slaughter. That they are suddenly expected to square stated goal with deed, when their whole professional life has been spent in the easeful shaded spaces in between. Call it hypocrisy, but that is the culture. They did not sign up to work in an abattoir.

Because who are the *known offenders*? Why, we round them up at the end of each month to pad out the arrest log, that is how come they are known. Sorry women too old or plain for profitable prostitution, who live at the edge of the slum and will fetch for a few banknotes and half a tablet for themselves, and who never had a few banknotes but gambled them away at simplified rummy in a leaky hut. Unemployable men, sullenly about their petty crime. And their feckless sons, with their doctored scooters, who live for the great free roar of the races on the outer ring roads on Saturday night—

'It is a headache,' sighs the superintendent, reclining in his sofa perhaps a little too comfortably.

'Yes,' says the minister. 'But it can be done.'

He is not sentimental. The equal value of all human life is a useful fiction, no more, and if you absolutely must kill to get a feeling of your power, it is better to kill those who benefit the common weal little or nothing. He was smug to think of himself as a man of principle. No doubt his fatal flaw, smugness. All he really has is a certain respect for the immutable truths that come to us in the teachings and are confirmed by our own common sense. One being that your actions should be proportional, and another that if you make a dragon, you must pay for it.

He looks his friend in the eye. 'I can be of no use to you.'

The superintendent smiles. 'For now.'

'For now. But my advice, for what it is worth—'

'Please.'

'—is that a declaration of loyalty to—' he flicks his fingers at an imaginary fly '—may compensate for a certain shortfall in the numbers.'

'Ah.'

'Not a great shortfall. You will have to produce, er, *results*. But it is difficult to get a clear shot in densely populated districts like yours. Nervous officers aim high—'

'Yes.'

'Start low, arrest a great many—'

'Oh, arrest is—'

'Quite. And fines.'

'Yes.'

'Fines on a scale that cannot be ignored.'

The superintendent lifts his chin as if to say that will be easy.

'Also, your association with me is known, so it will be worth all the more if you and yours are seen to come over to—'

The superintendent looks at him levelly. 'He will not trouble us forever.'

'No,' says the minister. 'But he will trouble us for a very long time.'

These, then, are his last days or weeks in office. He has run the gamut of the terrified officers in the corridors. 'Gently,' he has reassured them. 'Gently.' As if what is being asked of them were no more than a manoeuvring of obstacles that takes a sensitive hand on the steering wheel, and a tender foot on the pedals. But what more could he say, given that every word he says is even now being reported back to the Leader's people? In his official capacity he can be no use to these men for much longer, and some will soon enough regret coming here for reassurance.

Then the weekly press conference, with the flashing lights and the sudden impertinent questions. Is it true there is *conflict* between him and senior officials? No conflict, no, harmony reigns. Who would have briefed them? The blubber-lipped son of the south, with his tedious lists? That he is difficult, asks the same reporter, now emboldened, to work with? No more difficult than most, and perhaps less difficult than some, he said with a thin-lipped smile. This raised a titter among the journalists representing his core constituency, though others looked furious. We are essentially a nation, thought the minister, of football supporters, and our so-called free press the worst offenders. No, none of that put him off his stride.

Has he seen a certain video clip posted on the Internet? That question threw him, because he had not, and now it was the other lot's turn to titter. The minister put it to them, however, that he has better things to do than entertain himself with video clips, now that he is launching his new policy. The curfew, yes. It went down well enough among the reporters who represent his core constituency, but again there was a resistance he is not used to, a shifting sullen mass slightly to the left of centre. Did there exist a legal basis for such draconian steps? Oh indeed, talk about draconian steps! They are safer indoors with me than the lot of you outdoors with *him,* he felt like saying, but did not say.

And if it all lacked lustre, it nonetheless recovered perhaps a little ground, in the public eye; he had not then realised how urgently it needed recovering.

Back in the office he dismisses all flunkeys but his secretary and switches on the computer.

'The video clip?'

'Your Excellency—' The secretary is in acute pain again.

'Yes?'

'Well I would not—'

'You damn well would, and at any rate this is an order.'

Trembling, the man leans over the minister's shoulder and taps the keys. The minister shoves the mouse in his direction and pushes back his chair. The secretary clicks. It takes a lifetime to load, the clip, and the poor fellow's breathing becomes so laboured that the minister half-fears he will have to call an ambulance, this day of all days. But then it is up.

'Sound,' says the minister.

'Oh,' says the secretary and fumbles with the mouse.

A jaunty obscene ring-around country song, with clanking percussion and the one-stringed fiddle, to the effect that Little Brother, by the riverside, is down again and then up again, and then down again and then up again— The camera is on the minister, and before him a half-naked teenage girl, in a tiny skirt and a mere handkerchief over her puppy-fat front, and he is wagging his proud index finger at her to the beat. Then the camera pans away to find a pair of huge pink phallic windsocks, slowly tumescing and detumescing in the bright night; and the finger wags, and the teenage girl nods, and the windsocks tumesce and detumesce, and Little Brother up again and Little Brother down again—

The loop goes on for three-and-a-half minutes. He insists they watch it to the end.

24.

In the minivan, tired to the bone, chilled to the marrow, the minster shuts his eyes, but his ring-around mind will not let sleep come. Still, it is good to be ensconced here, in his plastic and vinyl box, and let the heaviness take his muscles. His work is nearly done after all, nearly done. They have skewered him so expertly that there is little day-to-day work left: it is his own constituency after all who will most ardently support the slaughter of the five thousand, give or take. That leaves such friends and acquaintances as he has overseas and in international organisations; discreet messages will have to be passed to them.

None of them are radically minded: he sees the error of his ways now. A wise politician makes contacts of every kind, but he has always stuck to more or less his own kind, abroad and in the international organisations, and truth be told at home too, to instinctive conservatives who do not raise a ruckus. And a ruckus will by and by have to be raised. Let us only hope that one or two can advise him where to turn. Let us hope that such supporters as he retains will be able to advise him which fires to stoke and where. The general perhaps, no doubt he maintains links with dissidents and malcontents—

No, he is very tired now. The avenues will open, by and by. He has at best a few weeks in nominal office. Already the press is turning on him, and the stories will proliferate in the columns: that he is difficult to work with, intractable, in conflict with senior officials, a hard, implacable presence around the corridors, the voice, when all is said and done, of unreason— Yes, it was well played, he has said it before and is already tired of saying it, to himself. He is already tired to the bone of the coming weeks, their wholly predictable course. By the time he resigns it will be gratefully, with a few dry words to the press, in their fake astonishment, their shrill hypocrisy, to the effect that more time must be spent with his family, and perhaps a long trip abroad. That will furnish him with opportunities.

It occurs to him only now that this is perhaps the best outcome for his best friend the superintendent. That this outcome may free the superintendent, with his mysterious powers and oddly static career, for the higher echelons at last. To the point where, had he told tales out of school to the Leader's people, it would not have been entirely unwise, nor even entirely unconscionable —

The minister is very tired now; tired of plotting and planning and divining motives behind the great veil of reality. He wants only, for now, to sleep, in a clean dry bleached motel room, with the girl at his breast —

But this is not the way. These are not the roads to the girl's apartment, and they are on the wrong side of the river. These grimy low facades are a hundred years old and have mouldings at the front. The clouds tower over low flat roofs. Motorcycles are piled high with crates or bolts of fabric. The traffic is thick, fast and disorderly. He barks at the driver, but the driver does not turn round. He knocks on the partition, but the driver stares straight ahead, implacable. He rattles the panes, but the partition is locked, with a safety lock he never noticed before. It gleams, in the icy interior. He beats the panes: bulletproof. He tries the doors: locked. The driver pulls the curtain shut.

Is it still not enough? Will they take me out now, in some abandoned godown in the old quarter, to be chewed by rats under a pile of wet rubbish? He is too tired, for the moment, to protest. It is out of his hands, everything out of his hands.

The thought comes to him how absurd he will feel, dying with dyed hair, roots showing, in front of hired goons. He wishes now he had not done it; there would be a dignity to his rag of a body if its hair was grey. It might follow one or the other of the hired goons into their sleep, that they murdered a venerable elder, and his grey hair soaking in a puddle. And yet what does it matter? Perhaps a little of the dye will seep—

No. They are officers, or ex-officers, like most hired goons in this country, and if he knows one thing it is to command officers. He will stall them, he will make them quail yet, he will—

The minivan stops. The kerbside door clunks and slides. The driver stands respectfully aside. Muggy air fills the minister's nostrils: fresh, muggy air, with a whiff of decay and rich green leaves. He hauls himself up by the handle and half-stands and steps out. His knee gives. The driver stretches a solicitous hand towards his elbow, but he shrugs it aside.

'*Rare!*'

The driver steps back as the minister straightens. They are at the gate of an old wooden house, so old that the garden has sunk a good few inches below the road. Great rain trees and flame trees reach out to the street with fanned fingers. The old sagging wooden gate is open and unsecured, and the driver motions for the minister to enter. He looks around: a still long dusty street, asleep. And where would he run? He enters. The driver shuts the gate behind him. The minister takes a few tentative steps down the path, which is old mossy herringbone brick, uneven, broken by roots in places. It has an untrodden look.

Out of the trees comes a spruce little hazy figure, all shiny in pink and silver, lithe on little feet.

'Your Excellency,' the person breathes as he comes closer. 'So very kind of you to come.'

'I did not—' the minister starts indignantly. But what is the point?

'You must forgive our little subterfuge,' says the little lithe man. The minister gets a whiff of floral perfume. He could have sworn the pink necktie caught a flash of sunlight in the stippled shade, so shiny is the starched silk.

'I must nothing. Who the hell are you?'

'Only your Excellency might have, in view of the—ah—*situation*, been as it were pursued, so we deemed it—ah—'

The minister, too late, remembers his phone, and plucks it roughly from his trouser pocket.

'That would not have worked,' says the sprite. 'The signal—'

'I am here. Get on with it.' His voice strikes him as boorishly loud, here in the restful stippled shade under the great trees, on the calm sunken path, in the presence of this soft gentle shiny creature. Still, it will not do to let them—

'Please your Excellency,' soothes the creature. 'If you would only step this way and—'

The minister shrugs. 'Fine.'

He is led across a pond and up a few springy wooden steps, through a cool dark musty traditional parlour or ante-room, with low seats and low tables on either side, across a raised courtyard and gallery, and along a corridor to a pair of magnificent old doors. The creature reverently opens them, bowing at the waist, and steps aside for the minister to enter.

The gloom beyond looks empty. There is a chair with a little table before it at eleven o'clock. The centre is taken up by a vast veiled palanquin or wedding bed. In the depth of the dark pitched ceiling flaps an ancient fan. A sacral smell of incense, and something else too, dry rot or damp, a kind of fungal invasion.

The blithe spirit points to the chair and the minister, overcome perhaps by fatigue or the temple atmosphere, sits meekly down. A second lithe creature, equally silky, brings a sweating frosted glass of iced tea or infusion on a little glass saucer, puts it down in front of him and retreats in a bowed position. The first lithe creature bows at the waist too and retreats, pulling the doors shut behind him.

Silence. He has not realised how thirsty he is and gulps down the cold watery tea in one. The glass rattles noisily on the saucer when he replaces it. He catches himself making a placating motion with his hand. He waits.

There comes from the depth of the room a sound like a soft whiffling fart.

The minister is not a religious man, not in the sense that he has ever had a supernatural experience. The ancestors, yes, he has paid his respects when required. He has tended to advocate the framework of religion, for the usual reasons. He has considered it useful. But his world has been purely material, suffused with no spirit, a collection of facts that might be so and so arranged, in order of usefulness. Not even for facts, in other words, has he felt any religious veneration. The great terrible it-ness of things of which he has heard speak—the bird-ness of birds, the dog-ness of dogs—that has not been his experience.

And yet as he sits here, in the presence of this vast wedding bed, the softly swaying curtains, and as his eyes adjust to the gloom, he senses rather than sees behind them a great bloated golden reclining presence. It is toad-like, elephantine, porcine,

215

all enormity and smooth vast bulges, and radiates an enormous sense of peace, or complacency; an enormous restfulness in itself.

It is without doubt quite dead, if it was ever alive. The room is a shrine, sacred to a past presence.

Yet as he peers and peers at the figure in the gloom, it seems to the minister as though he hears a voice: a voice that is at once like the breeze in the elephant grass, like the rain-prickle of the mud flats, like distant snarled evening traffic, like the clatter and clink and chatter of a thousand convivial meals. It seems to be speaking to him, or through him: oh, beautiful—a fluid rich playful voice, slightly sibilant, slightly oily in the overtones, and tremendously, preternaturally pleased with itself. And it says:

Hail and blessings. How very kind of you to come all this way.

Is some kind of response expected of him? Feeling foolish, the minister shifts his weight on the other buttock and tentatively clears his throat. No, the wrong kind of noise. Thought then:

What? thinks the minister.

Please do not be alarmed, says the voice.

I am not alarmed.

Of course not, says the voice. And it is that imperturbability in particular that we admire so very much about you, that steady—

Puzzled.

As who would not be? Let us, however, before we go any further, offer you our profound apologies, for what they may by and by be worth, for this whole unfortunate business, and our profound thanks also, for the excellent work that you have—

The minister snorts, mentally.

Please: the very excellent work that you have done, in the

very short time allotted. You have in a way become the very personification of order in the minds of many, our own not excluded. Henceforth, when we think of order, it is your good face that shall as it were rise before us like the morning star, or else the moon, some days before it is at its fullest, or some days after, it comes to the same thing.

The minister supposes he is fair game but does not see—

Please: we speak with the license perhaps of our great old antiquity, yet with great affection and, as we say, gratitude. But for your—

But for my nothing.

Oh no. Not at all. Already the superficial effects are everywhere apparent, but what is more, infinitely more, you dear good fellow—here a sound wafts through the room as of wind chimes being gently tickled by the breeze, a sound at once alarming and for all its condescension not unpleasant—your sacrifice, for make no mistake—

I did not sacrifice myself willingly, if that is what you think.

Are you so sure? You struck us from the start as a fellow—a dear, good fellow—well able to see himself within the context of larger forces, and moreover content to see himself in this way, which is the only way. For the individual, as you hardly need us to point out, is at once everything and nothing: to himself, everything; to the world, nothing. And yet there exist a rare few good fellows who are not, to themselves, everything, and therefore not, to the world, nothing: and among them we count you.

You flatter me—

—for a reason, dear one, for a reason. You do not mind the familiarity? We are so old now that even someone of your undoubtedly mature years, and of your somewhat, ah, reptilian appearance seems to us a mere dewy-cheeked child, a fledgling, a tadpole—

What I mind is of no importance, the question—

217

There you go again, with the selflessness.

You have brought me here—

Oh yes, to set your mind at rest.

At rest? Do you have any idea—

Oh yes. There is a sadness in the chimes and sighs of the voice now, a sense of measured sorrow and well-modulated grief. And yet, the voice continues, we would set your mind at rest. You have done—

Nothing. Thanks to whatever scheme—

Please. You pipe up and pipe up, admirably, to be sure, yet perhaps a little before time. It will not do, you see, to anticipate your elders and betters quite so rashly, because there may after all be something to be learnt, from your elders and betters, by simply holding your rash little tongue.

The scrape of cutlery and clatter of plates has become rather more pronounced in the soup of noises that makes up the disembodied voice. Before him, the bloated gold effigy gleams, immobile.

—but of course it is the privilege of men of action, such as yourself, says the voice, all wafting chimes again, to be rash. We too were once rash—

Oh?

Indeed. But let not ancient history distract us. What matters to men of action, such as yourself, is the Here, and the Now. So to business, as perhaps you might say.

The Leader—

Indeed. But has it occurred to you that he is so placed for a reason? That he is in a sense—an admittedly unpleasant sense—the Chosen One?

Chosen by whom? For what?

Our masters, as the great oiled iron wedge that will prise open our markets for international investment, so called. He is in a sense, is he not, a great historical force before which all others must yield? A thrusting ramrod of a thing. Oh beautiful, that by robbing one he should become the thrusting ramrod for all others—

Must yield? But the minister is blushing again. How stupid he had been to think he ever stood a chance. How abjectly stupid. But the slaughter—

Yes.

He will not hang for it.

Hang? No, we should not think so. Or be shot, or any of the many—

There we are.

But where, exactly, are we? Where is it written that he should hang? If you make a dragon, you must pay for it. That is all the ancient wisdom says. It does not specify the price, it does not—well, you know the rest.

I am no longer sure I believe the ancient wisdom.

But you must, my dear fellow, you must. It is only because of you that we have it at the forefront of our mind. Indeed we have a suspicion that there was no such ancient wisdom until you made it up.

I heard it somewhere— sighs the minister. He is very tired again.

Somewhere, somewhere, sings the voice. I heard it somewhere so it must be true, it must be you, it must be you. I heard it somewhere so it must be true, doobidoo, doopdeeloolah, doobidoo dopdeloolah, doobidoo—

It is only the fan flapping, thinks the minister, I have had so little sleep that the—

Sleep-de-beep, sleep-de-beep, sleep-de-beep, sings the voice, a sharp edge coming into it, like a cleaver. Sleep-de-beep bopdelooloah de-beep.

Or a radio—

When he comes to the voice is still warbling.

—and your part in it will no doubt be given its due, and the injustice done to you taken into account—

He rubs his face. It feels like a mask, greasy and insensate. Is that, he croaks—

—all? But my dear fellow, it is a great deal. It means, does it not, in one interpretation, that without your contribution to the harmonious whole there would have been—

He clears his throat. A lack, yes, I see now. I see.

The price will be paid. The voice is firm now, with a new booming undertone, a conch shell being blown in the distance. Oh, he will pay the price, never you fear. And this poor nation too will pay the price. There will be no rest for this poor nation for a long time to come, this poor guilty innocent nation, until every last coin has been deposited, with interest, in the relevant account. It is a terrible dragon we have made, a vile, contemptible beast. It is no better than vermin. We are scarcely better than dogs, and will be—

We? You did—

—nothing, yes. I could have risen, could I not, from the wedding bed? And I did not rise.

You could?

Or perhaps I could not, what does it matter? The impossible, to invent another proverb, needs no witnesses. Even so, would you like me to get up and dance? I am surprisingly nimble, despite this enormous bulk, on my ticklish old feet. Would that not be a sight? For I am also, behind these veils, quite naked. Only you see, my dear fellow, you could not then be allowed to live and tell the tale. You see? The impossible—

No witnesses, yes, I see.

Of course you do. And now—the voice is beginning to fade—we have entertained one another enough. At my great old age, you understand, one tires easily, one wearies of company, even delightful pond scum like you, and I am afraid—

But the minister can no longer make out the words. There are wind chimes in the distance, a breeze in the trees, a chirping of cicadas, and then nothing. It is quite dark now. There is the smell of incense and rot and stagnant water. A clatter of plates from some nearby house, televisions chattering of the day's events, a revving motorcycle. For a moment longer he sits, hands folded in his lap, peering into the dark depths behind the veils of the wedding bed. Then he braces himself against the backrest and with a tremendous effort gets up. Immediately the twin doors open wide, and a shaft of light comes in, and the silhouette of the lithe perfumed fellow against it, or another very like him.

A throat is being cleared.

'You are—'

'Quite ready, thank you.'

'It is this way.'

'Indeed.'

'Thank you. I have permitted myself to call your driver.'

'Thank you.' A glance at his well-faked watch tells him how late it is.

Acknowledgements

Somrak Sila, who told me many things. Jonathan Taylor, especially for his TIME cover story 'Speed Demons', March 5, 2001. Darkle for a beautiful cover. Woranart Vimolchalao, who told me the story of the Frog and the Little Fish. Siriporn Pongsurapipat for the motorway chase. Morm Chan Reaksmey for bits of robust wisdom. Ubolrat Thengtrirat, who knows all the sayings. None of them can be held responsible for my misrepresentations.

I may have stolen from Tom Plate's interviews with alleged Giants of Asia, *Doctor M: Operation Malaysia* and *Citizen Singapore: How to Build a Nation*, as well as the excellent *M.R. Kukrit Pramoj: His Wit and Wisdom*, eds Vilas Manivas and Steve Van Beek. 'One by one the guests arrive' is by Leonard Cohen. 'The lads in their hundreds' is *A Shropshire Lad* XXIII. The canal-boat wake is I think from *Arlington Park* by Rachel Cusk.

Copyright © 2018 by Nicolas Buchele
Cover photograph: Darkle
Cover design: Darkle

ISBN 978-3-9820152-0-0